BLOODLINE OF THE DRAGON GUARDIANS

Bloodline Of The Dragon Guardians

Book One
Destiny Awakened

Marta Vasquez

THIN LEAF PRESS | LOS ANGELES

Library of Congress Cataloging-in-Publication Data
Names: Vasquez, Marta
Bloodline of the Dragon Guardians. Book One: Destiny Awakened
LCCN: 2025921375

ISBN 978-1-968318-15-4 paperback) | 978-1-968318-14-7 (eBook)

Science Fiction Fantasy, Dragons, Coming of Age
Cover Design: 100 Covers
Interior Design: Dindo Sanguenza
Editor: Erik Seversen
Thin Leaf Press
Los Angeles

THIN
LEAF

PROLOGUE

GM paced back and forth in the dimly lit living room, his hands running through his hair as he muttered under his breath. His father, Ben, sat stiffly on the edge of the worn leather couch, while his grandmother rested in her usual worn-out rocking chair, her wrinkled hands folded tightly in her lap. The air was thick with tension; the only sound was the rhythmic creaking of the chair and the soft thud of GM's footsteps on the hardwood floor.

"Please, sit down," Ben said, his voice calm but strained. "We'll explain everything."

GM whirled around, his eyes flashing with anger. "Explain?" he snapped. "Explain what, exactly? That you've decided to offer up my child like some kind of sacrifice because of some ancient story? No, I won't let her take on this burden!" His chest heaved as he fought to steady his breath. "Besides, who even came up with this ridiculous idea? Why should I follow it? This prophecy is absurd ... I don't even know if it's true or just some twisted myth!"

His grandmother's gaze sharpened, but she said nothing. GM's hands curled into fists. "Have you ever seen anyone come out of those caves alive?" His voice cracked with desperation. "I would be sending my child to her death, and I can't do that."

Ben's eyes darkened, his jaw tightening. "It's not that simple."

GM shook his head, his heart pounding in his chest. "No. It's exactly that simple." The room fell into a heavy silence, broken only by the low hum of the storm gathering outside.

Ben stood up and took GM by the shoulders. "Son, you must take my word for it; know that anyone who enters the caves has willingly accepted their destiny; you will explain it to your daughter when the time comes. She is a strong, healthy, and very bright girl. She will understand and will do what is needed. Go home and speak to your wife; she will not take this lightly."

GM drove home, tears welling up in his eyes. He wiped them away and was determined to make Isa understand the prophecy; even though he didn't understand it himself, GM knew he must comply. Most of his apprehension came from what his wife's reaction would be. Would she accept what he was about to tell her, or would she protest?

PROPHECY

The time will come when the eldest son's middle child comes of age. She will rise as the guardian of the Earth Protectors, entrusted with the sacred duty of raising and guiding the next generation of dragon riders. They will be fearless and unwavering, their hearts bound by faith, their spirits forged in the fire of devotion.

They will soar across the skies with unwavering loyalty to Goel, their dragons mighty and resolute. They will stand as warriors of light, defending Earth against the forces of darkness. In the great battles to come, they will wield their strength in the name of Goel, striking down evil and restoring balance to the world.

And when the final storm has passed and the shadows of evil have been vanquished, peace and unity will again reign. Under their watchful eyes, the world will heal, and the prophecy will be fulfilled.

TABLE OF CONTENTS

CHAPTER ONE

Living on her father's farm was always an adventure for Martina. Being the middle child of nine, two brothers and six sisters, there was never a dull moment. Martina had long, dark brown hair, deep-brown eyes, and sun-kissed skin. Petite and slender like her sisters, she resembled them so closely that people often mixed them up.

But Martina stood apart in one significant way—there was something undeniable, something that set her apart from everyone else. It wasn't just the sharp intelligence in her eyes or the quiet confidence she carried, though those were unmistakable. It was something deeper, something almost intangible, like an unseen force that made the air shift when she walked into a room.

Where others accepted fate, she defied it. Perhaps it was the way she never flinched under pressure, how her mind worked fast, always anticipating, always seeing what others missed. Or maybe it was the way she carried secrets she didn't fully understand, etched into the fabric of her identity.

Whatever it was, it made her different. And in a world that feared the unknown, different was dangerous. Another thing that made her different and far less mysterious was that she hated wearing dresses, especially to church.

Sunday school class was the worst time to wear a dress. The stiff fabric, the way the lace collar chafed her neck, how the boys snickered and tugged at her braids when the nun wasn't looking. She refused to be an easy target. So she found a loophole. She'd wear pants under her dress, a quiet rebellion hidden beneath layers of fabric. That way, when class was over, she could chase them down without a second thought.

Her mother, Isa, caught on quickly. "If you don't wear the dress properly, you'll be grounded to your room all day," she warned, arms crossed, eyes sharp with the kind of authority only mothers possessed. In the end, Martina would put on the dress, stiff and uncomfortable, her scowl completing the look. But as she sat in church, listening to the sermon murmur on, she knew one thing for certain: she might wear the dress, but she'd never be the girl they wanted her to be.

Despite her mother's warnings, Martina preferred her jeans, hat, and worn cowboy boots—even if they pinched her feet. Dresses felt like a cage, stiff and uncomfortable, while her boots carried her where she wanted to go. Every morning, she braided her waist-length hair into two neat plaits, though she often fantasized about cutting it all off. The weight of it, the time it took, the way it marked her as the girl everyone expected her to be—it all made her itch for a pair of scissors. But the thought of her mother's reaction and the whipping she would get was the only thing that kept her hands at bay. For now, the braids and the dresses would have to stay.

The moment her morning chores were finished, Martina was out the door before her mother could think of another task to pile onto her. She didn't mind hard work, but she preferred dirt under her nails from the grease and soil, not from scrubbing floors.

She gravitated toward her father, watching him work beneath the hood of a truck or hunched over a broken tractor. Every clank of a wrench, every burst of steam from an engine, every calloused-handed repair fascinated her. She wanted to know everything, how to fix, how to build, how to make something broken work again. One day, she promised herself, she wouldn't just watch. She'd be right there beside him, elbow-deep in oil and sweat, proving she could do it too.

Martina's sisters were Willow, Marguerite, Magnolia, Meadow, Lena, and Gwynn; her brothers were Lukas and Phillipe. Martina and her siblings were close; other than disputes about some silly issue, they were her best friends. The girls played all day long; there were many ways to have fun and get in trouble when you lived on a farm.

Martina liked the family's dogs and cats, who were her constant companions as she made her rounds visiting the cattle and goats. No matter where she went on the farm, they eagerly followed at her heels. However, not all the animals were so friendly. The family also kept a flock of guinea hens, which Martina found terrifying. These feisty birds were aggressive, squawking loudly and chasing anyone who dared to come too close to their coop. To avoid their sharp beaks, claws, and relentless pursuit, Martina took no chances and would go out of her way, making a long detour around the barn, just to keep a safe distance from the vicious guineas.

The family loved their horse, an old but spirited gelding named Pinto. He was a striking paint horse, his coat a beautiful mix of deep brown and crisp white, with bold patches that made him stand out against the landscape. Despite his age, Martina and her siblings found a way to make him run like the wind: they would shake an empty bleach bottle filled with a few rocks to scare him, and off he went, thundering across the fields. His ears pinned back, nostrils flared, and his mane whipping wildly in the wind, lashing against Martina's face as she clung desperately to his coarse hair. She gripped his mane with all her strength, digging her heels into his sides, but no matter how hard she tried to stay on, Pinto was too fast. The moment always ended the same way—Martina tumbling to the ground, her skin scraped and bruised from the unforgiving earth.

Deep down, Martina hated it when they did this to Pinto. She worried his aging legs would give out or that he'd collapse from exhaustion. But Lukas had no such concerns. He pushed the horse to his limits, running him ragged through the fields, forcing him to leap over ditches as if he were still in his prime. And loyal as ever, poor old Pinto did exactly as he was told.

Fortunately, her father decided to give Pinto away. Over time, the once-loyal horse had grown aggressive, baring his teeth and lashing out with sharp kicks whenever anyone got too close. Deep down, Martina knew it was their fault; they had been too rough on their horse, pushing him beyond his limits. The guilt weighed on her, but she also felt relief. She would miss Pinto, but it comforted her knowing he was no longer at the mercy of their reckless games. At least now, he wouldn't have to endure the endless chasing, jumping, and exhaustion they had put him through. She hoped he had found a kinder home, where he could finally rest.

To keep themselves busy outdoors, the girls dug holes under the huge mesquite bushes; the roots made a great fortress! They would sneak a blanket out of the house for the defense; it was so cozy. Martina would fall asleep several times while playing under the mesquite fortress and wake to her mother hollering her name—what a fright that was!

Isa, their mother, was strict and always busy with the younger siblings, so Martina stayed clear of her whenever possible. Raising nine kids was difficult, and Isa took her motherly role seriously. If the girls were disobedient—for example, swimming in the canal when they weren't supposed to, or climbing the pecan trees and then jumping over to the roof of the house— Isa would line them up and give them a good scolding or worse. They never did learn that lesson; as soon as there was water in the canal, there went the girls, and the spankings quickly followed. Other times, when their mother left to shop for groceries, the girls would put on their roller skates and skate up and down the highway!

Their father, GM, was stern, yet Martina and her siblings respected and loved him dearly. He was a hard worker and expected the same from his children. Not once did Martina get a spanking from him, but when he was angry with them for causing their mother trouble, his facial expression was all the girls needed to start crying from the worry of disappointing their dad.

Their farm was beautiful, with alfalfa fields full of butterflies in the summertime. Martina and her sisters loved to sit and admire the land from the roof of the house; they would climb the pecan tree nearest the house to get to the rooftop. They could also lay out and get a nice tan with the sun rays beaming right at them. The girls would be two shades darker by the time they returned to school after summer break.

When the alfalfa reached its desired growth, GM would cut it with a windrower. The smell of cut hay was exhilarating to the senses. Martina wished she could bottle up the scent and take it out anytime. Once the cut hay dried and reached perfect humidity, a hay baler swooped up the cut-dried hay and shaped the grass into rectangular bales. As GM drove on, the baler would drop the hay bales in the fields, where Martina and her siblings would pick them up with hay hooks and place them onto a loader.

Once, Martina's hay hook got caught in the baling wire when she dropped the bale on the loader.

Martina rode halfway up the loader, dangling by one hand before she was able to release the glove and hook. She fell about ten feet, but other than a few scrapes and bruises, she was just fine. Her father shook his head in disapproval, and her sisters made fun of her for weeks. GM and Lukas would then stack the hay bales on the truck and take them to the barn. The hay was sold or given to the cattle, goats, and horses as food.

GM also grew cotton; throughout the summer, the family would cut weeds from the cotton and keep them at bay until harvest-time. Martina's father would then defoliate the cotton to dry the leaves out. Once the leaves dried up, fields of white cotton bolls were left. The white, fluffy stuff always reminded Martina of clouds or marshmallows. When it was harvesting time, her father used a cotton picker to separate the cotton from the boll and then dump it into a caged trailer. When the trailer was full, Martina and her siblings would climb the trailer, jump inside, and play for hours in the picked cotton. What fun they had!

These lands had been in their family for over 200 years and were passed on from generation to generation. Martina's great-grandfather had farmed only a portion of the land, enough to make a living and to put food on the table. The remainder was pastureland for cattle, sheep, and goats. The family also raised chickens, pigs, and rabbits for food. Martina's father bought the family farm after his father, Ben, passed away. GM was the eldest child in a family of 10; he was a hard-working man and highly respected in the small community of Loving.

Martina was ten years old when she started helping on the family farm. Her older brother Lukas, already working as a mechanic in the nearby town of Carlsbad, could no longer help with the farm work. That meant it was up to Martina and her four older sisters to step up and shoulder the responsibility alongside their father. The younger siblings would get their turn in the fields when they turned ten, but for now, Martina and her sisters carried the load.

Every morning, Martina and her sisters woke before dawn. After a quick breakfast, they'd head out to the farm, following the instructions their father had given them at the breakfast table. The work was hard—hauling feed, mending fences, caring for the garden vegetables, cutting weeds out of the cotton fields, and tending to the animals. The hot summer sun made it even harder. By August, Martina's tan had deepened to a rich brown, two shades darker than her usual color.

When school started again, the other kids teased her about her dark skin and rough hands. But Martina was tough. The first time someone called her a name, she raised her fists and warned them to back off. It took only one scuffle for the teasing to stop. After that, no one messed with Martina—not even the boys. Despite the hard work and teasing, Martina and her sisters took pride in what they did.

The farm was part of her, and she knew how to handle herself, whether it was in the field or on the playground.

CHAPTER TWO

When Martina was thirteen, she and her sisters were tasked with clearing rocks and mesquites from a newly plowed field, where their father planned to grow alfalfa. The work was grueling under the relentless summer sun, but it had to be done—the land needed to be free of large rocks before planting could begin.

Dressed in long-sleeved shirts and jeans, they wore the new bonnets their mother had sewn to shield their faces from the heat. Their oversized work gloves, though bulky, were essential for protecting their hands from jagged rocks and thorny mesquite branches.

Their father had given clear instructions: comb through the field, load the largest rocks into the truck bed, and haul them to a series of caves on another part of the farm. The caverns had become a hazard; several baby calves had fallen in and perished in their depths. Filling them with rocks was the only way to prevent further loss.

Week after week, the girls labored in the unforgiving heat—hauling stones, chopping down stubborn mesquite bushes, and tossing debris into the gaping holes of the earth. The work was backbreaking, their arms sore and blistered, but they pressed on. Each day, as the truck rumbled across the land carrying another heavy load of rock, they knew they were shaping the land not just for the alfalfa, but for the safety of the animals that roamed it.

One day, as Martina and her sisters hurled rocks into the caves, a sudden, cool breeze rose from the depths of one of the caverns. Martina stopped, brushed the sweat from her forehead, and turned to her sisters with wide eyes. "Sisters, can you feel that breeze?" she asked, stepping closer to the edge.

"Of course, I feel it," Willow replied. "The underground river runs through these caves. Dad told me about it years ago; that's how he gets water to irrigate the fields."

Martina frowned, glancing between her sisters and the cavern's dark mouth. "Well then, why are we closing the caves up? If there's a river down there, why don't we leave them open and go swimming?"

Her voice carried a note of excitement, and she took another step closer, peering down into the mysterious depths. The idea was too tempting to ignore. "Let's go check it out," she added, her voice turning conspiratorial. "Maybe it can be our new fortress!"

The sisters exchanged looks, part hesitation, part curiosity. The air from below was crisp and inviting, a stark contrast to the burning heat above. The thought of exploring an underground river, hidden beneath the very land they worked, sent a thrill through them. The question was … did they dare?

"No way, don't even think about it!" Marguerite hollered, her voice tinged with panic. "Mom will kill us if we go down there. She hates these caves, so we're covering them up, understand? Martina, you are never, ever going down there. Do you hear me? You could drown or get washed away and end up in Mexico!"

Martina rolled her eyes but gave a mock sigh, a smile tugging at the corner of her lips. "Okay, take it easy; I won't go down there… today…" she teased, trying to provoke her sister.

Marguerite shot her a sideways glance, her brow furrowing in frustration as she picked up another rock and threw it into the deep hole with a forceful toss. "You are impossible, Martina, you know that?" she muttered, eyes never leaving the cave's dark entrance. The rocks echoed as they hit the bottom of the cave, and the sound felt like a warning in the silence that followed.

Martina snickered, but the look on Marguerite's face made her swallow her sassy remark before it could escape. Her sister's expression was too serious and too scary to mess with. Instead, Martina simply watched as Marguerite continued working, her movements brisk and efficient but with an underlying tension. A question gnawed at the back of Martina's mind: What could be so dangerous about a place that had always been a part of their childhood?

They worked silently, unloading the last of the rocks from the truck bed. Then, without a word, they climbed back into the truck, ready to head to the fields for another load.

It took a couple of summers for the girls to clear several fields of rocks. It was a tedious task since the help of a backhoe or dynamite was needed to remove the enormous boulders. Whenever they went near the caves, Martina felt a yearning to go inside—she felt it to the roots of her hair and the tips of her toes. It felt like something was pulling at her chest, heart, and brain. She needed to go into that cave, and from that day forward, she plotted her excursion.

Martina was fifteen years old the summer she decided to explore the caves. It felt like the right time, the long-awaited moment when curiosity could no longer be ignored. Her oldest brother, Lukas, had often bragged about his brave adventure with their cousin, Mike, which had left them both shaken.

According to Lukas, they had ventured into the caves one day, only to encounter a terrifying creature that had sent them fleeing for their lives. His voice shook when he recounted the story, despite the years that had passed. After they had returned home, pale and wide-eyed, Lukas confessed their experience to their mother. In return, she had scolded him severely before sending him to bed without supper.

Yet, despite the stories, Martina couldn't shake the pull of curiosity. Filled with fear and excitement, she felt that this summer, the summer she turned sixteen, was the moment she had been waiting for. It wasn't just the story of the creature that fascinated her; it was the idea of experiencing something for herself, of stepping beyond the safety of the familiar, into the unknown.

The cave had always been forbidden, a place where danger lurked in the form of rattlesnakes and crumbling rock, and every adult had warned her against it. But those warnings only fueled her purpose. Now, old enough to make her own decisions, Martina was determined to uncover the truth. Was the creature real? Or had her brother's imagination run wild? Either way, she was resolved to find out.

To carry out this daring mission, she enlisted the help of her cousin, Anna, her closest companion. Though Anna was only four months older, they were as close as sisters, sharing a deep bond and an uncanny resemblance. With her straight brown hair and mischievous grin, Anna was the perfect partner for this secret expedition. Together, they were ready to face whatever the cave held, if it was even a place for the living to tread.

Martina and Anna had been inseparable since they were young. Anna's father was Martina's uncle, and their farms were not too far apart. Anna met Martina near the caves; Martina had brought her trusty dog, Silver, to guard them in case they found a creature. Silver could take him on; he was tough.

"Are you sure we won't get eaten by some wild animal?" Anna asked.

"Of course not," replied Martina. "There's no creature down there; my brother only made up that story to scare us."

"If we get eaten or killed, I will never come to visit you," exclaimed Anna.

"Okay, if we get eaten or killed, I'll forgive you for not visiting me," replied Martina. She tried to lighten their mood by saying, "Remember when we ran away from home?"

"Don't remind me," Anna groaned, rolling her eyes.

Martina couldn't help but smile at the memory. It had been years ago, but she still recalled the excitement, the planning, and, of course, the disaster that followed. It all started when they got in trouble for staying out past sunset. Their parents had grounded them, and in their youthful defiance, they had hatched a plan—they would run away.

They planned to live in Anna's late grandmother's house, which had been sitting empty for years; a perfect hideout, or so they thought. Martina had been saving up money for months, carefully stashing away every dollar she earned from chores and farmwork. With her savings and a roof over their heads, they were convinced they could make it on their own. Weeks of whispered conversations and careful preparations led up to their grand escape.

The night before, Martina packed her belongings in a plastic grocery bag and stashed it under the old bridge near the highway, safely hidden for the morning departure. She had thought of everything. Or so she believed.

At dawn, she crept outside, heart pounding with anticipation, only to freeze in horror. Her clothes—her carefully packed getaway gear—were scattered across the front yard like confetti. And there, in the middle of the mess, tail wagging proudly, was Silver. That crazy dog had found her stash and shredded the bag to pieces. Normally, Silver was a good dog; this time, he was a traitor.

Cursing under her breath, Martina scrambled to gather her belongings, stuffing them into a new bag before sneaking back inside. She couldn't let this setback ruin their plan. Later that morning, she and Anna met at the railroad tracks, their bikes loaded and their spirits high. Freedom was finally within reach. Or so they thought.

Barely two miles from home, Martina slammed on her brakes. Her money! She had left it behind, still tucked away in her room. Anna's face fell. "How are we supposed to survive without it?"

Martina sighed, shoulders slumping. "We better turn back."

And just like that, their grand escape ended before it truly began. They pedaled home in silence, knowing they could never speak of their spectacular failure.

But that was the thing about them … they knew how to keep each other's secrets. Both girls giggled, recalling the story, and prepared to explore the cave. Martina removed the sack she carried over her shoulder and pulled out a rope, flashlight, jug of water, knife, and the pellet gun she had taken from her father's shed. She had also packed a small blanket, matches, and some firewood. Anna took out the sandwiches and chips she had brought for lunch. Both girls giggled again as they noted their tools for survival.

The excursion was long due, and Martina had planned precisely what they needed. There was a risk of cave collapse, so Martina and Anna had brought matches to start a fire for warmth and to equip themselves against the creature.

CHAPTER THREE

Martina threw the sack over her shoulder but pulled out the pellet gun, loaded, and cocked it.

"Why are you doing that?" asked Anna. "You might shoot me in the back!"

"I wouldn't shoot you; I'm an expert with this guy," said Martina as she patted the side of the pellet gun. "Besides, I'm going in first. Here, you hold the knife, and don't stab me in the back with it!"

Again, both girls giggled, not knowing if it was out of fear or if the whole thing was funny. "We're going to be fine. Don't worry, we got this! Now let's go in and find us a creature to kill." Anna squinted her eyes and scrunched up her face, trying to look mean.

Martina laughed and made the same brave face. What would she do without her best friend?

Martina turned on the flashlight, and off they went, with Silver in the lead. With a mixture of excitement and fear, Martina and Anna crawled through the mouth of the cave, their flashlights cutting through the darkness like beacons of curiosity. The air was cool and damp, carrying echoes of past ages. The walls seemed to whisper secrets in Martina's ear, and the ground beneath them was a textured tapestry of dirt and uneven stone.

Animal bones littered the area, scattered haphazardly as if a predator had feasted there more than once. The air was thick with the scent of damp earth and decay. They moved slowly, each step deliberate, eyes scanning the uneven ground for the telltale movement or sound of snakes. The silence was suffocating, broken only by the occasional drip of water echoing through the cave.

Time seemed to stretch as they crawled forward, their hands scraping against the rough stone. Though it felt like hours, in reality, only minutes had passed. Then, as they ventured deeper, the narrow tunnel began to widen. Shadows retreated, unveiling a hidden chamber bathed in an eerie glow. At its heart lay an underground pond, its glassy surface reflecting the ceiling above like a portal to another world. Stalactites hung like frozen daggers, their tips mirrored perfectly in the water, and an unearthly stillness settled over the chamber as if it had been untouched for centuries.

The girls exchanged a glance, their wide eyes brimming with awe at the breathtaking sight before them. The cavern's hidden beauty was unlike anything they had ever seen.

"I think we better turn back," Anna whispered, her voice barely audible, as if she feared disturbing whatever unseen presence lurked in the shadows.

Martina, however, wasn't ready to retreat. "We've come this far; let's keep going," she whispered back, determination gleaming in her eyes. "Do you think there's a waterfall or something ahead? And what's with this mist all over our faces?"

By now, both girls' faces were damp, their clothes clinging to them from the thickening moisture in the air. A low, distant sound reached their ears, faint yet distinct. Martina froze, tilting her head. "Anna, listen! I think I hear running water. Can you hear that?"

Anna strained her ears, then nodded excitedly. "Yes, I can hear it!" She grabbed Martina's arm. "Let's keep going. Maybe there's an underground pool; we could even go for a swim!"

Their excitement propelled them forward, deeper into the cave. As they rounded a bend, the tunnel widened, and before them stretched a sight so stunning it stole their breath. A vast underground pond, nearly the size of an Olympic pool, sprawled across the cavern floor. Crystal-clear water shimmered, catching the golden rays of sunlight that streamed through cracks in the cave's ceiling. The surface rippled slightly, as though whispering an invitation.

Anna gasped. "Oh wow, Martina, look at this! We just discovered a magical pond!" Her voice was hushed, as if speaking too loudly might shatter the enchantment of the moment.

Martina's eyes sparkled with wonder. "Do you think we should go for a swim?" she asked, already stepping closer to the water's edge, entranced by the shimmering blue depths.

Martina and Anna had learned how to swim in her father's water well reservoir. It was as big as a small lake for all the family to enjoy every time Martina's father filled it up to irrigate the fields.

"Let's explore around first before we get in; I want to make sure the Loch Ness Monster isn't swimming in there," said Martina.

"Don't say stuff like that," exclaimed Anna. "That's not funny at all!"

Martina wrinkled her nose and stuck her tongue out at Anna, and they both laughed tentatively but then looked at each other with worry on their faces. They crept around the pond and noticed more bones from what looked like rabbits, and other bones from calves. Probably the calves that Martina's father had been searching for.

Both girls were accustomed to seeing dead animals since they were farm girls; they had to butcher chickens, rabbits, or those dreaded guinea hens for family meals. That was, after all, the reason they raised animals—for sustenance. They learned never to get attached to a rabbit, a chicken, or cattle.

Only trusty Silver, who had been unusually quiet, waited patiently by Martina's side. But as they reached the far edge of the pond, his demeanor changed. His ears perked up, his body stiffened, and a low, uneasy growl rumbled from his throat. Moments later, he let out a high-pitched whine, his tail tucked between his legs. Then, without warning, he spun around and bolted, racing back around the pond and out of the cave like a terrified rabbit.

"What the heck, Silver? Get back here!" Martina hollered, her voice echoing off the cavern walls. But Silver was gone, his paws barely touching the ground as he disappeared into the darkness.

Anna stared after him, wide-eyed. "Did he just leave us? Did he seriously ditch us?"

Martina swallowed hard, glancing around the cavern with sudden unease. "I don't like this. Silver's never acted like that before."

Anna's voice dropped to a whisper. "What did he see? Or hear?" She hugged her arms, a shiver running down her spine. "Why did he run like that?"

Silence pressed in around them, and for the first time since entering the cave, the beauty of the hidden pond no longer felt so inviting.

Martina's stomach tightened with unease. Silver was usually fearless, her loyal companion, always up for an adventure. Never had she known him to run from anything. But now, he was gone, bolting like a frightened pup.

Anna grabbed Martina's arm, her grip tight. "Let's get out of here, Martina. If something scared Silver, we have no business staying."

Martina hesitated, scanning the cavern, her instincts warring with her curiosity. "That's not like Silver to leave us like that," she murmured. "I wonder what scared him so much..." She took a cautious step forward. "Maybe if we go just a little further, we can find out—"

"NO!" Anna screeched, her voice slicing through the heavy silence. The sound bounced off the cavern walls, stretching into an eerie echo that made them both shudder. "Let's go NOW before we get killed!"

Martina swallowed hard, her pulse hammering. The shimmering pond, once mesmerizing, now seemed ominous, the mist curling over its surface like ghostly fingers. Whatever had spooked Silver was still out there, lurking unseen.

She exhaled sharply. "Okay… let's go."

Without another word, they turned and hurried back the way they had come, their footsteps quickening as the weight of the unknown pressed in around them.

As the girls retraced their steps out of the cave, they heard something: gravel underfoot, the sound of scratching on rocks. As they frantically looked around, trying to find the source of the sound, they saw a strange shape on the opposite side of the pond. What was that? Who was that? The figure stood up on its hind legs and screeched! It was the most bone-chilling, ear-piercing screech Martina had ever heard.

The girls took off at a run. Anna was first, Martina behind her with the pellet gun pointed back toward the cave, afraid the creature was following them. When they were almost out of the cave, Martina heard it. Someone called her name, almost like a whisper in her ear, the voice of a woman calling her: "Come back, Martina, I've been waiting for you; come back, you can't run forever."

"Run!" screamed Martina.

The girls scrambled toward the cave's entrance, crawling and clawing their way out, rocks scraping against their hands and knees. As soon as their feet hit the open ground, they sprang forward, muscles screaming as they tore through the fading light. They didn't slow until they reached the canal, doubling over, gasping for breath, their lungs ablaze. But the fear chasing them was relentless. Without a word, they pushed forward, running again until they reached the middle point between their houses.

Beneath the flickering embers of the dying sunset, they finally halted. The dusk pressed in around them, heavy with silence, the air thick with something unsaid.

Anna was the first to break the silence. "What the heck was that?" she cried, her voice trembling. "That was so scary. Was it a demon? I can't believe I let you persuade me to go there! What if it possessed us or, worse, cursed us?"

Martina stood frozen, her face pale, her eyes wide, locked on something unseen. She hadn't said a word since they escaped.

Anna stepped closer, her panic rising. "Are you okay? Say something. Are you hurt?" She frantically inspected Martina from head to toe, searching for scratches, bruises, any sign of what might be wrong. "What's the matter, cousin? Can't you talk? Have you been cursed?"

Finally, Martina spoke, her voice barely above a whisper, "Anna… did you hear it call my name?"

Anna stiffened. "What?"

Martina swallowed hard, her hands shaking. "It spoke to me. Right before we ran. It knew my name."

Anna's stomach twisted. "No. I didn't hear anything! All I heard was that horrible screeching. It was awful, I've never heard anything like it!"

Martina's breathing quickened, her fingers clenching into fists. "It said, *Martina… you can't run forever…* and it laughed. Anna, it laughed."

The setting sun played with them, its last golden rays flickering and fading, while a cold breeze slithered through the air, curling around them like an unseen ghost. Anna took a step back, her eyes darting around. "We-we need to go home. Right now."

Martina nodded stiffly, but as they turned to part ways, a faint yet unmistakable sound drifted through the air.

A whisper. A laugh.

And then, from the darkness behind them, a voice slithered through the air, dripping with something wicked.

"*Martina…*"

It was barely a whisper, yet it sank into their bones like ice. Both girls whimpered, clinging to each other as terror seized them. Were they just imagining the whisper or had they, in fact, heard it?

"What are we going to do? I hope it didn't follow us," Martina choked out.

"We will do and say nothing," Anna hissed, though panic crept into her tone. "If our parents find out we were there, we'll be grounded for the rest of our lives. But what if it…" she swallowed hard, "…what if that thing comes after us? What if it doesn't stop until it gets what it wants? What if it kills our family?" She shuddered. "We should never have gone in there. I knew it! I knew it!"

"Stop!" Martina pleaded, her voice sharp with fear. "You sound hysterical!"

Anna clamped a hand over her mouth, silencing herself, but her wide eyes gleamed with dread.

Martina's breath came in quick, shallow bursts. She glanced around, heart hammering. "Calm down, or we'll never be able to pretend nothing is wrong." Her voice was barely above a whisper, but every syllable quivered. "We better just go home… act normal… and say nothing. Just like you said."

But even as the words left her lips, the feeling of unseen eyes watching them lingered. Anna nodded, her breath still shaky. "Yeah… nothing happened. We never went there."

The girls exchanged a long, knowing look, their unspoken fear thick between them. Then, without another word, they pulled each other into a tight embrace, clinging to the comfort of familiarity for just a moment. As they pulled away, Martina gave a small, forced smile. "See you tomorrow?"

Anna nodded quickly. "Yeah… tomorrow."

Then, in an instant, they turned and sprinted off in opposite directions, their footsteps pounding against the ground. Their hurried breaths and leaves rustling were the only sounds breaking the eerie silence. Though they were a mile apart, within minutes, one thing was certain—neither would ever forget what they saw in that cave.

Martina turned back to see if Anna was okay; she was already out of sight. She continued running and didn't stop until she reached the canal near her house. She stood at the edge of the ditch and looked toward the house. Sitting on the porch waiting for her was Silver. "Coward," Martina called out at him. He whined, tucked in his tail, and hid in his doghouse.

Martina sat on the porch, running through the events that had just occurred. "What was that?" she asked aloud. To herself more than to anyone. She pictured the figure in her mind; she closed her eyes, and there in her mind, she saw the creature: a Lechuza, the Spanish name for an owl. Yet, it looked like an old woman. That thing had called her by name and said she had been waiting for her.

Martina ran her fingers through her hair and rubbed the tears out of her eyes. She walked inside the house, determined to speak to Lukas that evening when he got home from work.

CHAPTER FOUR

Martina never spoke with her brother about the cave, and her cousin Anna didn't want to come over for the remainder of the summer. She made excuses, saying her mother had her cleaning the house, that she was grounded, or that she had to work on the farm. Martina tried calling on the phone, and Anna's brother would say she was asleep or showering. Why was her cousin avoiding her? Was she still scared or mad about going into the cave? It was a long remainder of the summer without her best friend.

A month later, Martina turned sixteen and stepped into her junior year of high school, unaware that fate had already set her on a path that would shape the rest of her life. That year, she met the boy who would one day become her husband, the father of her children.

By eighteen, she had graduated, and their story took its next step. They married in a small ceremony filled with promise and youthful hope. It wasn't long before Martina discovered she was pregnant, a realization that both thrilled and terrified her.

When Angelica entered the world, Martina's heart was no longer hers. The moment she looked at her daughter, a love unlike anything she had ever known consumed her. Angelica was beautiful. Her big, soulful brown eyes held a depth far beyond her young age, and her dark, wavy hair framed her delicate face like a painting come to life.

Eighteen months later, Christopher arrived, perfectly completing their small family. He was a bundle of warmth and joy, with an insatiable curiosity that shone through his bright, intelligent eyes. His chubby little hands grasped at the world around him, eager to explore; to Martina, he was the handsomest baby boy she had ever seen.

Motherhood changed everything. It anchored her, reshaped her dreams, and filled her with a purpose she hadn't even realized she was searching for.

Martina felt truly blessed; Goel had gifted her two extraordinary, healthy children. She vowed to be the best mother she could be, to shield them from harm and give them a life filled with love and warmth. Nothing mattered more than her children; she would do whatever it took to keep them safe. Martina stayed home with the kids until Angelica turned four. But by then, a gnawing sense of unease had settled deep in her bones; her marriage was unraveling, thread by thread. She knew she couldn't rely on it to hold. She needed stability, a way to protect her children, and a future she could control.

Determined, she enrolled in beauty college to become a hairstylist. Every late-night study session, every exhausted morning, was driven by a quiet, growing fear, not just of an uncertain marriage but of something far older, something that still haunted the edges of her memory.

When she earned her cosmetology degree, Martina wasted no time. She opened her own beauty salon in the small neighboring city of Loving, carving out a livelihood that ensured she could support her children independently. It was hard work, but she thrived, finding comfort in routine, in scissors snipping and blow-dryers humming.

Yet, no amount of success could erase the past.

Whenever she visited her parents, she kept her distance from the caves. She never spoke of them, never mentioned the creature. Even after all these years, she could still hear the way it had whispered her name from the shadows, a sound she would carry with her forever.

In the years that followed, Martina and her cousin Anna drifted apart. Life pulled them in different directions—Anna married, had children, and eventually moved away to Colorado, putting even more distance between them. She rarely visited, only coming back for the holidays, and when she did, neither of them spoke of it. The creature remained an unspoken wound between them, festering in silence. But their bond was never the same.

Martina often wondered if stepping into that cave had been a curse. It had to be. Not only had she lost her best friend, but, at times, she felt as though she had lost pieces of herself, her sense of peace, her certainty in what was real.

Several years later, she finally ended her failing marriage. It had been a mistake from the start, a slow unraveling she had ignored for too long. The only good that had ever come from it was Angelica and Christopher, her greatest blessings, two shining lights in the lingering darkness.

Martina continued working as a hairstylist to make ends meet until she met Marcus at a family reunion; it was love at first sight. They dated for about a year, married, then Martina and the kids moved to Texas with Marcus. He worked in the oilfield, and they lived in different cities depending on where the company relocated them. He helped raise Angelica and Christopher; the children grew up, graduated from high school, and joined the military after graduation. She was so proud of her children.

Martina would visit Loving a few times a year to see her parents and siblings; they were getting older, and her mother was not in good health. The years passed, and Martina and Marcus worked, lived, vacationed, and visited the kids. They had a good life together. Angelica met her husband, Nate, in the military and fell in love; he was the perfect match for her. They married and had a beautiful daughter named Theris, and she meant the world to Martina. Theris had dark wavy hair, dark eyes, and the most beautiful smile Martina had ever seen. She and Marcus would fly to California for weeks just to be close to their granddaughter.

When Martina turned fifty, her mother became gravely ill, and she and her sisters had to care for her in the last days of her life. While their mother lay on her dying bed, Meadow called all the girls outside to show them an owl perched on the tree outside their mother's room. It sat there, just watching them with no fear at all. The eerie look in its eyes gave them shivers. Willow persuaded everyone to go back inside and leave the creature alone.

The next night, Martina sat outside breathing in the cool night air; she lay back, stretched out on the driveway, and watched the stars in the dark sky. She felt like she could see the entire galaxy in the clear skies; she was on a planet of her own, and there were no worries, no concerns.

While Martina lay on the driveway, a giant owl landed on her stomach, pinning her to the spot! Martina was too terrified to move, fearing the owl would rip her open with its talons. The owl looked at her and spoke—not spoke, but mentally communicated with her. "The Lechuza waits for you to return to the caves; it will take your mother tonight if you do not return." And just like that, the owl flew off!

Martina was too shocked to move, too stunned to say a word. She jumped up and ran into the house, out of breath, screaming at the top of her lungs, "The owl from the tree just spoke to me; it told me to go to the cave; the owl told me Mom would die if I didn't go!"

Martina's sisters looked at each other and burst out laughing. "What are you talking about?" said Willow. "Have you lost your mind? Now you can speak with owls?" They laughed so much that Martina became annoyed with them and went to her mother's room.

She sat at her mother's bedside and said, "Mom, I know you can't hear me anymore and don't understand me, but I must tell you something. When I was fifteen…" She tearfully told her mom the story about the creature in the cave, and the owl, and how it had mentally communicated with her to go see the Lechuza.

Martina's mother had been unresponsive for days, yet once she finished the story, her mother slowly turned to Martina and said, "Don't go to the Lechuza. She will make you take her place in la Cueva de la bruja, the witch's cave!"

Martina gasped. "What do you mean, take her place, Mom? What are you talking about?"

Her mother took a long, deep breath, took one last look at Martina, and was gone. Martina held her mother's hand, crying and willing her to wake and tell her about this Lechuza in the cave. Had her mother been delusional in the last moments of her life, or was Martina in for an adventure she didn't want to have?

The next few days were a blur, with funeral preparations, rosary, and burial. At the funeral, Anna approached Martina. "I'm so sorry for your loss, cousin. Is there anything I can do?"

Martina looked up at Anna with a tear-streaked face. "I've missed you so much. Anna, you are my cousin and best friend, but you stopped coming over and talking to me. We had a plan; we would always live close to each other when we married and had kids, and it all changed because of the cave. Why?"

Without a word, Anna turned around and was gone. The look on her face was not anger; it was more like fear. The same look she had had when they got out of the cave at fifteen years old.

Martina sat there for hours after everyone left the cemetery. She didn't even attend the reception afterward. Had her mother said a Lechuza or a witch was in the cave? Or was she the same? Martina recalled the figure she had seen in the cave many years ago; it had looked like an owl, or was it a witch? The feelings of desperation all swarmed back into her mind. But her father had blocked all entrances with huge boulders many years before. Even if Martina had wanted to return there, which she didn't, she couldn't get into the cave.

Martina didn't return to the cave; there were too many people in her life to consider. She had Marcus and her children, her granddaughter; she would not risk everything to do… what, visit a witch? She returned to Texas, resumed her life with Marcus, and tried to push it all to the back of her mind. She never mentioned the owl to Marcus or her children.

CHAPTER FIVE

Martina was now fifty-three years old, and her daughter Angelica had blessed her with another grandchild, a son named Bennett. He was such a handsome boy, with bright eyes that sparkled with curiosity and a smile that could light up any room. Martina instantly fell in love with him.

Angelica and her husband, Nate, were both in the military, and their lives were filled with purpose and joy. They were happy, a family united in their shared commitment, and Martina couldn't help but feel a deep sense of pride for them.

Her son, Christopher, had spent fifteen years in the military before transitioning to civilian life. He had moved back to Texas and settled in Abilene, just a few hours away from Midland. Now in college, he was pursuing his dream of becoming an engineer. Martina felt an overwhelming sense of pride for him too. Her children were thriving, carving out their futures with determination and success. Life was good for them all.

There was no reason for Martina to return to Loving for a while. She kept in touch with her father, called him regularly, and stayed connected with her sisters through text messages. But despite the peace she had built for herself, a nagging question still lingered in her mind … why had the owl chosen her? Why was she the only one it had spoken to?

But it was time to bury that incident deep in the folds of her mind, where it could stay locked away. It was time to move on, to leave the past behind, and to live her life to the fullest, surrounded by the love of her children and the quiet joys of the present.

Several more years passed, and Martina's health declined. She had developed several genetic illnesses—arthritis and diabetes, not to mention weight gain; she had gained so much weight from depression and lack of exercise. But she continued with her life until the day her beloved Marcus died. Martina could not bear to live in their home of 30 years after his death. She sold the house and decided to spend part of her time with Christopher and the other time with Angelica, Nate, and the children. Martina helped with the grandkids, picking them up from school and taking them to the park. She adored her time with the grandchildren.

After several months, her eldest sister, Willow, invited Martina to New Mexico for a visit. Little did Martina know that her life would never be the same again.

Returning to her hometown was nothing like Martina had expected. She hadn't set foot there since her mother had passed away, and the weight of that absence still lingered in the air. Her father had since died, but she hadn't been able to make it to his funeral, claiming it was due to her health. The truth, however, was far darker … she was terrified. Terrified of returning to the farm, terrified that the owl might appear again, or worse, she would come face-to-face with la bruja. The fear of those old, haunting memories was a shadow that followed her even into the safety of her adult life, and she wasn't sure she was ready to confront them.

Martina finally returned to New Mexico and the farm that had shaped so much of her childhood. Her brother, Phillipe, had inherited the land after their father's passing, and to her quiet relief, he had honored it well.

The vast rows of cotton stretched toward the horizon in neat, sun-drenched lines, and the lush green alfalfa fields swayed gently in the breeze, just as they had when she was a girl. The familiar scent of earth, warmed by the afternoon sun, filled her lungs. Martina stood in silence for a moment, taking it all in.

The land was still alive—still beautiful—and thriving under Phillipe's careful hand. Pride stirred in her chest, mingled with a deep, unexpected longing. As she looked over the fields, her heart whispered what she hadn't yet dared to say aloud: this place still felt like home.

Martina would go on daily walks with her sister, Willow; they spent the days relaxing near the pool at Willow's house and enjoying the warm summer. The two women would laugh and joke about the past, and Willow would poke fun at Martina about the owl. She was too old and tired to get mad, so she would laugh it off and try not to let it get under her skin.

"Why don't you move back to Loving full-time?" asked Willow one day as they floated in the pool. "Leave your kids be and let them move on with their lives."

"They enjoy having me there, and I love being with them," said Martina.

But the seed of doubt had been planted; she did have land that her father had given her years ago, and she had enough money to build a home if needed. "You can live here with me," said Willow.

"No, I can't do that; you have your children and grandchildren that come to visit," said Martina. "Not to mention that I have my children and grandchild that need me."

"Well, you shouldn't impose on your kids either," stated Willow.

Martina somewhat agreed with her sister, but the mere thought of not living with Angelica or Christopher made her heart ache. She loved being around her kids and grandkids and didn't want to think of a future where she would live away from them. She put the thought to the back of her mind and went to her sister, Magnolia's, house, where they had a few drinks and snacks. The other sisters came over with their grandkids, filled the swimming pools with water, and watched the kids play while the sisters reminisced about old times.

The following day, Martina decided to walk on the farm and have herself a long think. Willow's children had come for a visit, and Martina didn't want to be in the way. She had so many things on her mind and wanted to ponder what her beloved sister had said. She thought about her children and grandchildren and what she wanted to do with her life. That's when Martina stopped, dead in her tracks; she looked up and realized she somehow had gotten off the main trail and had ended up right in front of the cave entrance.

The cave beckoned her to enter; she dared not! Had all this been a dream so long ago that she had concocted in her mind? Martina decided to call Anna, who had moved back to Loving several years before to care for her ailing father. "Hello?" responded Anna.

"Hey, it's me, Martina. I've been thinking about you, cousin, and I miss you. There's something important I need to discuss with you. Can you meet me at Dad's land, by the ditch near the old well? You remember; that was always our secret spot when we were kids."

"What do you mean? Are you telling me you are near the cave where we saw the demon? Martina, that creature almost killed us at that cave! What is wrong with you? Why are you there? Martina, get away from there; that place is evil!" Anna hollered. She was hysterical and screaming over the phone. Martina couldn't comprehend half of what Anna was saying.

"Calm down, Anna; I'm not going in. I want us to talk and catch up."

"Well then, come by my dad's house; why meet there, of all places? Why there? That place is why we aren't close; that place is why I have nightmares every night; that place is why I never go near any cave dwelling! Cousin, please, get away from there!" Anna was inconsolable.

Martina told Anna that she would come by her father's house, and they could visit.

Martina continued to sit outside the cave as dusk descended, the cool evening air heavy with a noticeable unease, a presence that gnawed at the edges of her mind, impossible to ignore. Oddly, though, despite the disquiet that clawed at her, being here, in this place so tied to her childhood, offered a strange comfort. The flood of old memories seemed like a refuge, a place where she could hide from the unsettling truth she couldn't face. Yet, there was something beneath the surface of those memories—a whispering, something that felt like it was pulling her deeper into the shadows of the cave. She finally concluded that she was losing her grip on reality.

With a sharp, frustrated sigh, Martina stood, her legs stiff from sitting so long, ready to leave this haunting place behind and return to the familiarity of Willow's house. But as she rose, a shadow detached itself from the cave's black mouth—a massive owl, larger than any she had ever seen. It shot out from the darkness like a phantom, its wings beating with unnatural power, and landed on a large rock across from her. Its golden eyes locked onto hers with an intensity that felt like a presence in itself, a gaze that didn't just see but knew, beckoning her toward something hidden in the dark.

Martina glared at the owl, her frustration boiling over. She wanted it to speak. She needed it to explain what it was, why it had brought her here. The silence between them stretched, heavy and charged, as she willed the owl to respond.

Then, it screeched a bone-chilling sound that vibrated through her skull, like claws scraping against stone. Her vision blurred for a moment, and suddenly, a voice—cold, commanding, like the distant echo of the cave itself—pierced her thoughts. "Come inside and see the Lechuza," it whispered into her mind.

A cold shiver cascaded down her spine. Martina hissed, her voice a low, avenging whisper, "Who is Lechuza, and why does she want to see me? What is this madness? Why should I go there?" Her chest tightened, her pulse quickened, and the owl's gaze remained unblinking, unwavering. The air between them thickened, saturated with an eerie, unspoken tension.

The owl's eyes narrowed, and the voice from the cave grew darker, deeper, like the wind through the hollowed stone, "She calls you, Martina. She has always called you. Come and see what she waits for."

And then, Martina felt it.

The presence.

From deep within the cave, it wasn't just the owl now; in the shadows, there was something else. It watched her, and she could feel its eyes burning into her soul. La Bruja de la Cueva.

Martina's breath caught in her throat; her pulse thundered in her ears. For years, she had wondered why the Lechuza had called for her. Why did this thing, this presence, haunt her with its beckoning? Had it always been this way? Had she always been meant to walk into the shadows of the cave? Did it want her life? Her soul? Her blood?

She could feel it, that pull urging her to step forward into the waiting darkness.

But that was enough.

Martina's mind snapped into focus. She wasn't a puppet to be manipulated. She was done playing by their rules, done being dragged around by forces she didn't understand. This would end tonight. She was going to face the truth, whatever it was.

Her chest tightened with a newfound resolve. She took a step forward, each movement deliberate, her heart steadying in her chest. She would not be cowed. Martina had had enough—she would settle this mystery once and for all but on her terms and not Lechuza's!

Martina left, walked straight to Willow's house, showered, dressed, and walked to Anna's father's house. She knocked on the door, and after a few seconds, Anna answered. Her face was ashen; she showed her fear and uneasiness around Martina. She wished they had never gone to that place when they were teenagers.

"What... what are you doing here?" asked Anna tentatively.

"It's time we talked; can I come in, or are you coming out?" Martina had let this indifference go on for too many years. Granted, they had lived miles apart for most of their adult lives, but it was 2027, and cell phones were a life necessity. No more excuses. It was time to settle their dispute.

Anna stepped onto the porch, crossed her arms, and watched Martina. A look of disdain and uncertainty was on her face. "I didn't go in if that's what you're wondering," Martina exclaimed. "I have a lot to tell you before you say anything."

"I don't want to hear it; it's the devil's work. I don't know why you were at that place. We both saw that creature that day, yet you keep returning there. It's the devil, I tell you, the devil!"

"Anna, let me explain something. I have been drawn to the cave ever since I can remember, even as a kid, when we had to throw rocks in the holes. I always felt a force pulling me toward the caves. Kind of like I needed to go in there; I can't explain why; I just had to see for myself."

Anna shook her head, ran her fingers through her hair, and rubbed her temples.

Martina continued, "There's more, Anna; please listen. When my mother was dying…" Martina continued to tell Anna the story about the owl, the Lechuza, and what her mother had said. Anna's face drained of all color; Martina could see her terror. "Listen, I will never rest or be at peace if I don't know what the Lechuza wants. I have lived with this curse or whatever it is my entire life; what if it passes on to my children?"

Anna somewhat listened, yet when Martina finished speaking and stood up to hug Anna, she shrank away. "Goodbye, Martina. Don't come back here if you see the creature; it's a demon and will possess you if it hasn't already. That's probably the reason you are so drawn to that place." Anna turned and opened the door to go inside. Before she closed the door, Anna said, "If you do go into the cave, don't come over here again. I must protect my family." She closed the door behind her.

Broken-hearted, Martina walked back to Willow's house; she couldn't believe Anna didn't want anything to do with her. Martina went to her room; she was tired and needed to sleep but instead began to make plans for the following day.

CHAPTER SIX

The following morning, Martina dressed in her hiking clothes and rummaged through Willow's garage for a backpack and other necessary supplies. She packed a flashlight, extra batteries, snacks, water, and the 9mm gun from her purse; she was ready to finish this. The cave was a couple of miles away; Martina could have driven there but decided maybe the long walk would help her change her mind about entering the cave before she got there, but the walk to the cave only gave her more conviction to settle this. She prayed all the way there for strength, mercy, and resolution. She prayed Goel would protect her on her mission to find answers.

The buzzing sounds of the cicadas in the distance had Martina on edge; they made a similar rattling sound as a rattlesnake. She needed to be cautious this time of year; you never knew when a snake would hide under a rock to escape the heat. The sun was high in the sky and hot in the summer months, and the terrain in New Mexico was dry and desert-like. Martina pushed through the thick mesquite bushes and tangled brush, the hum of the nearby cave echoing deep in her chest. Each step felt heavier as the sound grew louder, drawing her closer to its source.

When she finally cleared the overgrown thicket that had long hidden the cave's entrance, the air grew cooler and a damp, musty scent filled her nostrils. She paused for a moment, the odor mixing with the earthy tang of the desert, sending a shiver down her spine. The cave emerged before her, an eerie void of darkness, its mouth like a gaping wound in the earth. Despite the unsettling sensation crawling up her skin, Martina's resolve did not waver. She had come this far and she wasn't about to turn back.

She checked the perimeter once more, scanning for any signs of movement or danger. Her sharp eyes saw nothing but the stillness of the desert around her. Taking a steadying breath, she reached for the large rocks blocking the cave's entrance, her muscles straining as she cleared them one by one. The noise of the stones scraping against the rough earth echoed in the silence, but Martina didn't flinch.

With the final rock pushed aside, she dropped to her knees and crawled into the cave, her body trembling in anticipation. The air grew colder inside, the sound of her own breath mingling with the distant hum. Every inch she moved felt like an eternity, but her curiosity and the promise of whatever secrets lay within drove her onward. There was no turning back now.

Martina whispered another prayer to Goel, seeking protection as she stepped deeper into the cave. Her eyes flicked upward, and she flinched slightly when she noticed the cave ceiling crawling with pale, skittering creatures. Crickets. The sight of them made her stomach turn. These were white or cave crickets, their spindly legs and eerie appearance evoking the image of spiders. Though mostly harmless, their unsettling presence never failed to send a shiver down her spine.

As she pressed forward, Martina's flashlight beam revealed scorch marks etched along the cave walls. Her fingers brushed over the burns, a chill creeping down her back. What could have caused this? The marks were old, their edges frayed, but something about them seemed unfamiliar, even though she'd been here as a child with Anna. Had they missed these signs all those years ago, or were they newly formed? The thought lingered uneasily in her mind.

With the flashlight in one hand and her 9mm in the other, Martina continued deeper into the cave. The light flickered as it danced across the jagged walls, and she felt the space around her expanding. The passageway widened, and soon, she could stand upright, her head no longer brushing the low ceiling. But the deeper she went, the longer the walk seemed, each step feeling more deliberate, more drawn-out. The cool mist she and Anna had felt years ago was gone, replaced by an overpowering stillness that made her skin prickle. Still, she pressed on, her heart pounding with the realization that this was no longer a childhood adventure—it was something far more dangerous— and she couldn't afford to turn back now.

The cave was silent, so every step was taken with caution. Then, a cool breeze, fog, and the sound of a nearby waterfall added to the ambiance. Martina tapped at the flashlight, but it kept flickering. She stopped, removed her backpack, and searched for the backup flashlight. It was not the time to be left without any light. Martina noticed slimy walls, mossy surfaces, and damp clothes as she walked through the cave. When she reached the lake, now larger than she remembered, she saw it … the Lechuza … standing directly across from her.

Martina's heart pounded as she questioned her sanity but kept walking toward the strange figure. Cautiously, Martina approached the creature and saw it was an older woman covered in feathers with long, silver, unkempt hair. The woman's unpleasant smell made Martina feel sick. They stared at each other in silence until the Lechuza approached her, tears visible in the woman's eyes. Martina stepped toward the crying woman and recognized her. Martina's heart raced as her mind scrambled to place the woman's face. The features were so familiar, yet distant. Then it hit her, like a bolt of lightning: this was the face of her great-grandmother, Lala.

Martina gasped, her breath catching in her throat. "Mama Lala, is that you?" Martina's voice trembled, almost unrecognizable as it echoed in the cavernous space.

The woman cleared her throat, the sound echoing off the stone walls like the rattle of bones. "Yes, it's me. I am Magala D. Basquez, your great-grandmother."

Martina's mind reeled, her thoughts spiraling. "It can't be. You…you died when I was just a child," she whispered, her voice cracking as memories from years ago flooded back.

Magala's eyes, dark and unfathomable, bore into her with an unsettling calm. "No, that was the story you heard. But I did not die. Your grandfather wanted everyone to believe I was dead… but I am well, and very much alive."

Martina's pulse thundered in her ears. "Are you saying they faked your death? Why would they do that? Why are you here, and why do you look like this?" Her voice wavered as she gestured at the woman's appearance—her skin too pale, her eyes too sharp, her very presence too unnatural.

Magala's lips curled into a faint, knowing smile. "Sit, and I will explain."

But Martina remained standing, her legs like lead, her heart pounding so violently she thought it might burst. Her mind screamed with questions, but one burned through her thoughts, relentless and sharp. "Before I listen to anything you say," she started, her voice rising, "I need to know … did you have anything to do with my mom's death? The owl told me… told me that if I didn't come here, she would die. And then… she died, minutes later!"

Martina's breath hitched as she stumbled forward, a burst of adrenaline rushing through her veins. "Are you a witch? A demon? Did you curse my family? What are you?" Her hands shook uncontrollably, her chest tight with hysteria. She could feel the walls closing in on her, the dark cavern pressing down on her, suffocating her. All she wanted was to bolt, to escape the weight of this moment.

The urge to flee burned in her limbs; she felt like she could sprint out of the cave and never look back, have the place bulldozed or, better yet, dynamited into oblivion. But something rooted her to the spot, her body betraying her instinct to run. She couldn't move. Not yet. The silence stretched between them, thick and oppressive, as if the very air in the cave was holding its breath.

Lala's gaze never wavered as she studied Martina, her eyes dark and piercing. Suddenly, a soft flutter filled the air, and Martina's heart skipped a beat as the owl, the same one that had spoken to her earlier, swooped down from the shadows and landed gracefully on Lala's shoulder. Martina's breath caught in her throat. What the heck? This woman, this thing, was no mere mortal. She was a witch. No, worse... something darker.

Panic surged through Martina. This was her chance; she couldn't stay here a second longer. Her legs pumped into action as she sprinted toward the exit, her heartbeat thundering in her chest. But just as she neared the cave's opening, the owl flapped its wings and shot directly in front of her, blocking her escape with its terrifying, unblinking gaze.

Martina held the gun firmly in her hand. It felt cold and heavy in her grip, but it was the only thing standing between her and whatever this nightmare was. The owl didn't budge. Her finger hovered over the trigger, ready to fire if the creature didn't move.

Lala's voice broke the tension, calm and measured, "I am not a demon, Martina. Nor a witch. And you are not cursed. I swear to you, neither I nor anyone else had a hand in your mother's death."

Martina's pulse raced, but she didn't lower the gun. She couldn't. Her gaze flicked between Lala and the owl, her thoughts tumbling in chaos. "Then why did the owl tell me to come? Why did it lead me here?" Her voice trembled with the weight of the questions, but the fear in her eyes was unmistakable.

Lala's expression softened slightly, though there was an undeniable weight to her words. "Many years ago, when I entered this cave, I made a choice. I chose the creature I loved most to stay with me, to hunt for me. I had always admired the owl's ability to fly and to hunt in the dark. Its hoot, its grace, its beauty, its very presence captivated me."

Martina's eyes flickered with confusion, but she didn't lower the gun. The air between them thickened with a sense of inevitability.

Lala's voice grew gentler, but there was an edge to it. "Your mother's death was inevitable, Martina. It was her time. Goel was ready for her."

Martina's throat tightened as the weight of Lala's words sank in. She shook her head, barely able to keep the gun steady. "So, you're saying that you had nothing to do with it? That you didn't—"

"No," Lala interrupted, her tone more insistent. "I had nothing to do with your mother's death. The owl was only trying to guide you here, to help you understand. To help you embrace the truth of what you are, of what you're meant to become."

Martina stared at her, disbelief clouding her thoughts. "What do you mean? What I'm meant to become?" Her voice faltered. "What truth?"

Lala's gaze softened with a strange sorrow. "When you take my place, a spiritual animal will enter the cave with you, just as the owl did for me."

Martina froze, the cold air of the cave pressing against her skin like a vice. "Take your place?" Her voice cracked. "Why would I want to take your place here, in this horrible place?"

Her heart pounded harder now as if her body knew what the words meant before her mind could fully process them. No. She couldn't... "Why would anyone choose this?" Martina whispered, the horror of it sinking in like a stone in her gut.

Lala took a slow step forward, her presence immense. "Martina, please. Sit, and I will explain everything about the prophecy, and tell you why it's your destiny, why it's always been your destiny."

The shadows in the cave seemed to grow longer, the weight of Lala's words pressing on her chest. Every part of Martina's being screamed to run, but some force, some unseen force, kept her rooted to the spot. She couldn't turn back now, not with the truth so close.

But what truth? What kind of life was this woman offering her?

Lala's silver hair cascaded like a waterfall down her back, a testament to the years she had spent tending to a legacy that stretched beyond memory. Lala's eyes held the wisdom of countless lifetimes; each crease was a story etched into her skin.

Martina saw the sincerity on the woman's face and decided to listen to her story. Martina's legs felt shaky under her and she didn't know if she could take another step anyway.

CHAPTER SEVEN

Lala's voice dropped to a soft, deliberate murmur as she began. "Our story goes back many generations, Martina. It begins with your great-great-great-grandfather, Bascal Derdjanian." She paused, letting the name linger in the air, heavy with weight. "Bascal, his wife, and their five children were among the last of their kind, Martina, they were dragon riders. They migrated here, fleeing from Shaytan, the evil one, and the dangers that followed them." Her eyes darkened, the shadows in the cave seeming to creep closer. "Assassins were sent to hunt them, to kill their dragons. To destroy them."

Martina blinked, trying to process the words. Her mind struggled to reconcile what she was hearing with the reality of the world she knew. "Dragon riders? Now I've heard it all!" She laughed bitterly, doubt coloring her tone, but there was a chill settling in her gut that made the words taste wrong on her tongue.

Lala's gaze never wavered, her expression solemn. "I know this sounds impossible to you, but it's the truth. The dragons were not legends, Martina, they were real, as real as the blood in your veins." She stepped closer, her shadow stretching long across the cave's walls. "Bascal and his family didn't just ride dragons, they bonded with them, lived alongside them.

They were protectors, guardians, gifted with abilities that have long since faded from the world."

Martina's breath hitched, the weight of Lala's words sinking deeper. Dragons? Protectors? Guardians? She could feel her heart pounding, each beat resonating through the silence of the cave. This was too much. Too insane. Yet, something in her gut told her that every word Lala spoke was grounded in a dark, twisted reality.

Lala continued, her voice low, almost conspiratorial, "But their enemies weren't just human assassins. Shaytan sent creatures and dark forces to destroy them. And, ultimately, they succeeded. Bascal's family was forced to scatter, to hide. But Bascal knew something that would keep his lineage safe."

Martina narrowed her eyes, her grip tightening on the gun. "What do you mean? What did he know?"

Lala's eyes gleamed with a strange light. "He knew that the bloodline of the dragon riders had to be preserved. And so, he made a choice—to create a place where his descendants could hide from those who would seek to end them. A place… like this cave."

Martina's pulse quickened. The cave? Her mind reeled as the pieces began to fall into place. The owl, the warnings, her mother's death—it was all tied together, somehow.

"You're saying this cave… it's part of some legacy?" Martina asked, her voice tight with disbelief.

Lala nodded slowly, the weight of her words pressing in like the walls of the cave. "Yes. The cave is a sanctuary, a holding place. And you, Martina, you are the middle child of the eldest son and the last in the bloodline of the guardians. You are the one who must carry the legacy forward and fulfill the prophecy." She let the words hang between them, heavy with implication. "You will become the next protector. Just as Bascal did before you, as I do now. And when the time comes, a spiritual animal will come to you, just as the owl came to me."

Martina took an instinctive step back, her mind reeling. A spiritual animal? Guardian? Dragons? These words kept running in her mind.

Her gaze flickered to the owl, perched silently on Lala's shoulder, its eyes watching her with an unsettling passion. The air seemed to thicken, each breath she took feeling like it might be her last. The walls of the cave felt closer now, pressing in on her as though they were alive. The reality of the situation was closing in … her reality.

"You're asking me to take your place, to live here, in this cave… with dragons? No, Lala. That's insane. I'm not a protector. I'm just… just a woman trying to survive!" Martina's voice wavered, panic clawing at her throat.

Lala's face softened, a sadness in her eyes that Martina could almost feel in her bones. "I'm not asking you to live here forever, Martina. But the time is coming when you will have to choose. Your destiny awaits, whether you embrace it or run from it. The choice is yours, but the bloodline cannot fade. The dragons must live on."

Martina's mind raced as the cold grip of fear tightened around her chest. The thought of becoming something she didn't understand—something tied to dragons, to ancient secrets, to death—was overwhelming.

But Lala's words lingered, impossible to ignore. "You are the last," Lala repeated softly. "You are the only one who can continue the legacy."

Martina felt her legs weakening, her hand trembling as she gripped the gun. Was this some twisted fate she had no choice but to accept?

And then, through the chaos in her mind, one thought cut through like a jagged knife. The cave wasn't just a sanctuary, it was a prison. The weight of that realization hit Martina like a punch to the gut, jolting her out of the fog that had clouded her thoughts. Her breath came sharp, her pulse raced.

"This is the most ridiculous thing I've ever heard!" she exclaimed, her voice trembling but defiant. "Dragons have been extinct for hundreds of years. You're telling me they still exist, here, in this cave?"

Lala's face remained calm, but there was an unmistakable urgency in her eyes. "Listen to me, Martina. Many years ago, it was not uncommon to see dragons soaring through the skies. They were fierce, majestic creatures, and the Derdjanian family had the most incredible dragons of them all. The bond between rider and dragon was unlike anything you can imagine. They communicated telepathically, a connection forged by faith in Goel. It was through that bond that peace was maintained."

Martina stared at her in disbelief, every word sounding more fantastical than the last. But Lala wasn't finished.

"Dragons helped keep peace in the land, but peace doesn't last forever. War broke out. Destruction spread like wildfire. And when the dust settled, the fear of dragons grew; they became a poison in the hearts of men. People began to see the dragons not as protectors but as threats. They feared what they couldn't control. And so, they hunted them. They hunted us." Lala's voice trembled with the weight of the past, but her eyes burned with fierce clarity.

Martina's mind raced, trying to absorb the impossible. "So, you're saying... men hunted dragons to extinction?"

"Yes," Lala replied, her voice low, almost grief-stricken. "The dragons were driven into hiding, moved into underground caves, far from the reach of men. But the hunters were relentless, they tracked the dragons and hunted them down. Eventually, the dragons were cornered and their sanctuary was discovered. All but two were killed." Her voice dropped, becoming a whisper as her eyes met Martina's. "Bascal's sons, your ancestors, protected those two remaining dragons with their lives. They fought to their last breath to keep the dragons safe.”

"And so, Bascal’s journey began with a sense of urgency and a determined resolve. He chartered a ship, braving the vast ocean with his family and the two dragons, seeking a new home where his loved ones could finally live in peace. The dragons, a secret he and his family could never fully share with the world, were their most precious protectors, and Bascal knew they couldn’t afford to be discovered.

"Once they reached North America, Bascal set out on a difficult search for their new sanctuary. By day, he and his wife, along with three of their children, traveled by wagon, carefully crossing the unfamiliar land. But at night, the dragons soared through the skies, avoiding the gaze of any who might look too closely. The dragons’ senses were unparalleled vision that could pierce the darkness and scenting abilities so keen that they could track Bascal’s presence from miles away, no matter where he traveled. Their bond was unbreakable.

"Bascal’s faith in Goel guided him. It was through prayer, through the quiet whispers of his heart, that he found the city of Loving—a secluded, peaceful place far removed from the threats they had left behind. After purchasing one thousand acres of land, Bascal and his family moved swiftly, taking the dragons into the underground caves where they could remain hidden, their protection finally secured. Here, in the shadow of those ancient tunnels, they would finally be safe.

"Among the dragons, one stood out above all—the majestic Shincari. Her size was monumental, her scales shimmering with a thousand hues in the moonlight, and her eyes glowed with an eerie intelligence. She was fierce, and yet, beneath her formidable exterior, she held a deep, unwavering loyalty. To Bascal's sons, she was not just a dragon, but a family member, one who had protected them since they were children. Her bond with them was as strong as their blood.

"Shincari and her mate, Haragarph, lived for many years within the caverns, keeping the land safe from all who would dare to challenge their legacy. It was in these caves that Shincari laid her eggs, and though her life eventually waned, her purpose was fulfilled. Her final moments were spent in the company of those she loved most, her fierce spirit finally giving way to time.

"But before she passed, Shincari called Benlasio, one of Bascal's sons, her rider and closest companion. With her final breath, she entrusted him with the sacred task of guarding her eggs. They would not hatch for any rider, but for the new riders, the ones who would one day return to the land, as foretold by the prophecy. The eggs were not just a symbol of hope, but a promise, one that would be fulfilled when the legacy of the dragon riders returned to the earth.

"Haragarph, too, felt the loss of Shincari deeply. Her death had shattered him, but the bond between them had been so deep, so eternal, that his sorrow consumed him until he too passed away, guarding the last remnants of the dragons' legacy. The caves, once a life sanctuary, now lay dormant, waiting in silence for the day the eggs would hatch and the new riders would emerge.

"The prophecy, however, wasn't just a legend, it was a call. As the years passed, the memory of the dragons faded into myth; it waited, hidden beneath the earth, deep within the caves, awaiting the return of the dragon riders who would once again rise to defend the land.

"Our family has sworn an oath to protect Shincari's eggs for generations. Today, Martina, you join that sacred legacy. Soon, you will be the guardian of these eggs. A spiritual protector will remain with you within the cave, ensuring their safety. The essence of the dragons keeps us alive, granting us many years. The cave's unique atmospheric pressure enriches the air, oxygenating your blood and sustaining life. The guardian cannot leave this place, for the elements are deadly outside the shelter.

"When Shincari lived, she shed countless scales. These scales, imbued with powerful healing properties, cure wounds and ailments of all kinds. You will feel their presence here, woven into the very fabric of this sacred place. The ponds here provide fish, but should you desire other meat, our spiritual companion may leave the cave to hunt."

Lala's voice held the weight of knowledge, yet amidst these tales of old, Martina stood still, her mind swirling with disbelief. The notion of dragons seemed far removed from reality, nothing more than a fantastical story spun from myth and imagination, and she refused to be swayed by such legends.

But Martina's heart remained tied to the tangible, to the reality she knew. "I won't be part of this," she declared, her voice tinged with a determination that allowed no argument. "Dragon eggs are hidden away in caves! It's absurd. I have a life to live beyond these tales."

Her grandmother, Lala, regarded Martina with empathy and patience. "Child, the world is vast, and what you deny now will one day hold the key to your purpose. Listen with your heart, and you will hear Shincari's voice."

Martina's gaze hardened, her stance unyielding. Tradition and destiny hung heavily, but she would not be persuaded. Martina looked at her surroundings, inhaling deeply and exhaling slowly. Amidst the echoes of her steadfast skepticism, a tremor coursed through Martina's senses. A whisper of something ancient and mysterious brushed against her consciousness, like a gentle touch from a world she had vowed not to believe in. Her steps weakened, uncertainty and curiosity warring within her as the sensation intensified, a beckoning she couldn't ignore.

CHAPTER EIGHT

In the silence of the caves, the air seemed to hum with an enthusiasm that dared explanation. It was as if the foundation of reality was shifting, revealing a truth beyond Martina's perception. And within that current of unseen energy, a presence emerged—intangible yet undeniable. Martina's heart quickened, a strange mingling of fear and intrigue taking hold. Her gaze swept the surroundings, but there was no physical form to attach to the sensation surrounding her. It was as if the cave held its breath, awaiting her response.

"Who's there?" she finally called out, her voice full of defiance and curiosity. The sensation deepened—a subtle reassurance woven into the currents of energy that now surrounded her. And then, like a whisper through the wind, a name brushed against the edges of her consciousness: *Shincari.*

A shiver raced down Martina's spine, her skepticism fighting with the mysterious connection she felt in that single word. Shincari—a name that held weight beyond its syllables and resonated in the spaces between belief and disbelief. For a fleeting moment, Martina's doubt about Shincari's existence dissolved. The caverns seemed to exhale a moment of stillness before the world transformed. In her heart, Martina knew this was no mere illusion or trick of the mind.

The presence was real, and in its touch, she felt the threads of destiny she could no longer deny.

Lala spoke again, her voice steady with the weight of tradition, "The calling of the guardian began with Mangalia, one of your ancestors, the middle child of five. It was decreed that the firstborn would always yield their middle child to the caves, bound by duty to protect the eggs. Mangalia followed this path, and when she had children of her own, her firstborn would give up their middle child to take her place. And so, the cycle continued generation after generation.

"Mangalia's granddaughter eventually took her place, and after many years, the duty passed to me. I was the middle child," Lala continued, her eyes dark with memory. "But I was also known as Magala. My firstborn son died, and with his passing, the burden fell to the next generation—your father, GM, the firstborn, who must give up his middle child. And now, Martina, that child is you. You will take my place until the day the riders return, the day of reckoning, and the return of Goel."

Martina sat frozen, her mind reeling. This was madness. A tale ripped straight from a storybook—fantasy, fiction, the stuff of myth. How could she possibly believe that she was destined to guard dragon eggs?

Impossible! "This is completely and unbelievably ridiculous," protested Martina. "There is no way that I am going to live in this gross and smelly cave the rest of my life, and I cannot believe anything you are telling me." Martina stood up and paced around the pond. "Why would I do this? Why would I give up my life to protect dragon eggs! Which, by the way, I have yet to see! Not to mention my children and grandchildren; what would they think if I just disappeared off the face of the earth to live out the remainder of my days in this place?"

A wave of dizziness washed over Martina and she sank to the ground. Sensing her distress, Lala stepped forward cautiously. "Come with me," she said gently. "I will show you the eggs, and then you will understand what must be done."

Despite the whirlwind of emotions, Martina's curiosity flared. She forced herself to stand and followed Lala around the pond, deeper into the labyrinth of caves. How far had they traveled? The passage twisted and turned, each new cavern blending into the next, until they reached an opening bathed in a mesmerizing glow of orange, red, and gold.

Heat radiated from within, wrapping around Martina like a living thing. Did Lala keep a fire here to stay warm? But as she stepped inside, the truth struck her breathless.

At the center of the chamber lay a vast, nest-like hollow filled with smoldering coals and what looked like a bed of molten lava. And nestled within it—fourteen enormous eggs, their scaled surfaces shimmering with an array of brilliant colors.

Martina stood frozen, unable to tear her gaze away. They were magnificent, unreal. A part of her still clung to disbelief, but another deeper part of her whispered—*this is real*.

Lala's voice took on an almost reverent tone as she stepped closer. "Martina, you are of the Derdjanian bloodline. You are the middle child of the eldest Basquez son, destined to be the next guardian of the Bascal Derdjanian dragons. Your children and grandchildren will one day stand against doom, destruction, and total annihilation.

"The end of days will come, Martina, it is only a matter of time. You and your descendants must be ready. You must protect Goel's people from ruin, from the darkness that the evil one and mankind will unleash upon this earth. Your lineage has been chosen. Your children, and their children after them, will be dragon riders!"

Martina's heart pounded in her chest. What the heck…

Her breath came in shallow gasps as the walls of the cavern seemed to close in. She shook her head violently, trying to reject the impossible. She squatted down, fingers tangling in her hair, but the room was spinning, whirling in a dizzying blur of heat and light.

A wave of nausea crashed over her, rising like a tide she couldn't fight. The edges of her vision darkened.

And then … everything went black.

Martina woke on a cot-like structure and a warm blanket covering her; next to her were some nuts and berries on a wooden plank. Also next to that were the snacks that she had brought with her. Alongside was her 9mm, which she immediately grabbed and checked to ensure there was still ammo. It was loaded and ready to go. She drank from one of her water bottles but had no appetite; she began to assess her surroundings.

Martina stood and walked out of the room. She went into a large cavern with a waterfall coming from the side of the rock. The area was enormous, as big as the entire city of Loving. How had Martina or her family not realized that this cavern had been down here the whole time? She remembered the Carlsbad Caverns she had visited as a child and the immense size of it. The entire population of Texas could live there!

But the cavern where Martina stood was vast, twice the size of any she had seen before and ten times more breathtaking. Towering stalagmites rose from the ground like ancient spires, while delicate stalactites dripped from the ceiling, glistening like frozen daggers. Flowstone cascaded down the walls in graceful, curtain-like formations, their rippling layers resembling folds of fabric carved from stone.

Everywhere, the cave sparkled with diamond-like crystals embedded in the rock. The faint light trickling in from above struck their facets, igniting a mesmerizing display of colors that danced across the cavern walls in a shimmering, ethereal glow.

Martina could only stand in awe, utterly speechless.

Lala cautiously approached her. "Martina, you must go back and teach your children the way of the dragons. Show them how to have faith, to believe in Goel, to become warriors—dragon riders!"

Martina's eyes widened in confusion. "Go back? What do you mean, back? My children have lives, and families. They do have faith and believe in Goel as their savior but they're not warriors! And dragon riders? How could I possibly teach them that?"

Panic gripped her chest, her breathing quick and shallow. A familiar nausea churned in her stomach and bile rose to the back of her throat. She barely made it to the corner of the cave before she vomited up the water she had just swallowed.

Tears burned her cheeks as she shook her head, overwhelmed. But then—warmth. A gentle hand rested on her shoulder, radiating an unexpected calm. The storm within her stilled, if only for a moment.

"Martina, your parents should have told you the truth about your destiny as the guardian of the Derdjanian dragon eggs. You were meant to raise your children as warriors, training them in archery, swordsmanship, and every form of combat. But your mother forbade your father from telling you. And now, here we are."

Lala's gaze darkened. "Much has changed because of their mistake. But there's no time to dwell on the past, only to fix it. Tell me, what year do you wish to return to?"

Martina's breath caught in her throat. "Return?" she echoed, voice barely above a whisper.

"It must be after your children were born, yet early enough for you to train them in the ways of the dragon. Let me think…" Lala paused, deep in thought.

Martina's heart pounded. What in the world was Lala talking about? Go back in time? That was fantasy storybook nonsense! And if it were possible, it would mean returning to the darkest period of her life, back to the man who had caused her so much pain. No. She couldn't. She wouldn't.

She turned on her heel, ready to leave the cave, to walk away from this madness.

But Lala was faster. Anticipating Martina's resistance, she seized her arm and placed both hands on either side of her head.

A flood of visions crashed into Martina's mind—flames engulfing cities, the clash of swords, the screams of the dying. She saw herself, her children, and generations of their offspring falling beneath the weight of war and destruction.

They would all die if Martina didn't take her place as the guardian of the dragon eggs!

Martina gasped, her knees nearly buckling. The choice was no longer hers alone.

Cyberwarfare would cripple the government, plunging nations into chaos. Critical systems would collapse, including power grids, communication networks, and national defenses—all rendered useless. World War III was no longer a possibility—it was inevitable.

The visions struck Martina like a physical blow. She fell to her knees, sobs wracking her body as despair consumed her. Her heart ached with the weight of approaching catastrophe. When? She wondered through her tears. When would this devastation unfold?

Yet deep in her soul, she already knew the answer. She knew what had to be done. But how could she possibly achieve it?

Lala's voice rang with urgency, "You will return to 1988. Your children will be young enough to train and prepare for what is coming. Seek me out when you arrive, and I will explain more then."

Martina's breath hitched. 1988… back to that life? Back to… *him*?

Lala placed a firm hand on her shoulder, her voice unwavering. "You will remember everything. Your memories will remain intact. This is your chance, Martina. You can change your story. You can change the fate of this world."

A pulse of energy surged through the cave. The air crackled.

"NOW GO!"

Martina looked up at Lala, her vision blurred by lingering tears. Lala's arms moved in sweeping arcs as she chanted in a language Martina had never heard before—ancient, powerful, and thrumming with energy.

Suddenly, the cave lurched. The walls twisted and warped as if the very fabric of reality were unraveling. Martina's stomach dropped. A force pulled her backward, yanking her through a spiraling tunnel of color—blue, green, yellow—blending and flashing in a rapid sequence.

Her mind reeled. *Am I dreaming? Did I pass out again?*

She tumbled through the endless void, weightless, disoriented, slipping in and out of consciousness. The rushing wind roared in her ears, then…silence.

A tiny hand tugged at her nightgown. "Wake up, Mama! I'm hungry!"

Martina's eyes snapped open. Blinking against the soft morning light filtering through an old curtain, she found herself lying in a small, familiar bed. Her breath caught in her throat.

A three-year-old stood beside her, wide-eyed and impatient.

Her child. She was back.

CHAPTER NINE

Martina blinked, then blinked again. She rubbed her eyes and looked into the most beautiful little face she had ever seen. Her daughter, Angelica, was three years old. Martina got out of bed, picked Angelica up, embraced her daughter, and repeatedly kissed her beautiful little face. She rubbed her nose with Angelica's and gave her butterfly kisses. Martina's heart swelled with love. Angelica giggled and hugged her mama, then wiggled out of her hands and proceeded to the kitchen for breakfast.

A sound stirred behind her, slow, steady breathing.

Martina's body tensed. A cold shiver crept up her spine as she turned her head slightly. There he was, her ex-husband, lying on the opposite side of the bed.

A wave of nausea crashed over her. Her pulse pounded in her ears as she took in his sleeping form, his face relaxed in ignorance. This man was the bane of her existence. The thorn in her heel. She despised this man. How was this real?

The bile rose in her throat, hot and bitter. She barely made it to the bathroom before collapsing over the toilet, retching violently. Her stomach twisted, heaving out the sheer horror of her situation.

Panting, Martina stumbled to the sink, gripping it as if it were the only thing tethering her to reality. What the heck? Her heart pounded against her ribs. Was this real? Had she gone back in time, or was this some cruel nightmare?

She turned on the faucet, splashing cold water on her face before rinsing out the bitter taste of bile. Bracing herself, she lifted her head.

Her reflection stared back at her in the dim light. Her breath hitched.

She was young again.

Her long, dark hair was thick and healthy and cascaded over her shoulders. Her skin was smooth and glowing with youth. And her body, oh my goodness. She ran her hands down her arms and over her waist, feeling the firmness and lightness. She was tiny, strong, and twenty-two again.

A shiver crawled down her spine. *Lala actually did it. She sent me back.*

Martina staggered backward, gripping the edge of the counter. She would have to do it all over again—the heartbreak, the struggle, the choices. Could she endure reliving her twenties, knowing what was coming?

A sharp jolt of anger cut through the confusion. That dang Lala hadn't even given her a choice. She exhaled shakily and dropped onto the toilet, pressing her palms against her temples. She had to think. Had to act.

And then she heard it. A deep, groggy sigh from the bedroom. A rustling of sheets. Martina's stomach clenched. She had to get out before he woke up. The very thought of seeing his face, of hearing his voice, made her skin crawl. She couldn't stay here. Not another second. She had to escape. Now.

Martina heard a cry from the other room; her son Christopher must be in his crib. He should be about two years old now. Christopher was so young and so beautiful. This was Martina's handsome, striking, and strong son. His big eyes looked up at Martina and he raised his arms; Martina picked Christopher up and hugged him. He snuggled in her neck, putting his arms around his mama. Martina cried. Her tears would not stop, they flowed like a river longing to be set free.

The emotions in Martina were so overwhelming that she almost felt herself floating in the air. Now, when Martina thought she could no longer stand, she felt her daughter Angelica pulling on her nightgown with a quizzical expression. "Mama crying, don't cry, mama."

Oh, Mija, I missed you and your brother so much. Martina bent down and picked Angelica up with her free arm. She propped Angelica on one hip and Christopher on the other and walked to the kitchen and fed them both. Martina sat there watching them eat; her children were her life—they always had been. Martina would do anything to protect them; today was the day to change her future and her children's.

Instantly, Martina knew what had to be done. She left the kids eating, headed to the bedroom, and packed her suitcase with everything she could fit in her bag. She packed another bag with Angelica and Christopher's clothes and shoes. Martina went outside, put the suitcases and bags in the car, then ran back inside, dressed herself and the children, and headed to her parents' farm before the loathsome man lying in bed woke up.

As Martina and the kids drove off, she looked in the rearview mirror at her old house. Her ex had never done anything to improve their house, yard, or lives. Nine years she was married to that man, nine years of misery. It was time to change her life. Goel had granted her a second chance—a rare gift she could not waste. This was her chance to set things right, to reshape the future, and to give her children the lives they truly deserved.

Her heart raced as the weight of it all settled in. This wasn't just about herself anymore. This was bigger. Much bigger.

Now, she had to face the ones who could help her understand it all—her parents. It was time to talk to them about Lala, the dragons, and the destiny she had never known. The truth would come out and she would finally be prepared to embrace the role she was born to fulfill.

The future of her children—and the world—depended on it.

Martina arrived at her parents' home, her heart heavy with emotions. Just hours ago, she had been convinced her parents were gone forever, but now, here they were, alive and well. She stepped inside with her children, and there, at the kitchen table, her parents were having breakfast. Angelica and Christopher, full of joy, rushed over to their grandparents and enveloped them in hugs. Martina stood frozen, speechless, her heart aching with a mix of disbelief and overwhelming love.

"Martina, what are you doing here so early? Are you okay?" her mother asked, concern in her voice.

Without warning, Martina ran into her mother's arms, clinging to her as tears welled up in her eyes. "Oh, Mom, I've missed you so much," she whispered, her voice breaking. She then turned to her father, wrapping her arms around him too, unable to contain the flood of emotion.

"Martina, what's wrong? Are you okay? Did that pendejo hurt you again?" her father demanded, his tone sharp as he quickly moved toward her, inspecting her face with concern. He cupped her cheeks in his hands, and the sight of his worry made Martina break down completely.

"Dad, can I come home?" she sobbed. "I don't want to be married to him anymore. I'm going to divorce him. I'm so sorry I ever married him, but I'm ready to change my life. Can the kids and I live here with you? I'll go to college, get my degree, and then we'll find our own place."

Her voice shook with sincerity as she added, "I want to make you proud of me, Dad. I won't disappoint you. I promise I'll be a better daughter to you and Mom. I'll do it right this time."

Her parents exchanged a quiet, knowing glance, then looked back at her. With warm smiles, they nodded in unison and enveloped her in a tight embrace.

"Welcome home, Mija," they said in unison, their voices overflowing with love and relief.

In that moment, Martina felt a surge of warmth wash over her. She knew, without a doubt, that she had made the right decision.

There were still four siblings living at home, but Martina was determined to make it work. They settled around the kitchen table, sharing breakfast, and as the conversation flowed, Martina promised her parents that she would explain everything in more detail soon. "I just need to take care of a few things first," she said quietly, her mind already racing with what needed to be done.

It had already been a long morning, filled with so much emotion, so she laid the kids down for a nap to give herself a brief moment to plan her next move. Then, with a sense of quiet resolve, she drove into Carlsbad. Her first stop was the family attorney's office, where she filed for divorce. Deep down, she knew her husband had no intention of changing—he had never changed. She had been saving money since the start of their marriage, squirreling away every dollar she could, and now, those savings were enough to cover the cost of the attorney's fees.

Once that chapter was set in motion, she made her way to the local college. She walked in, feeling a mix of excitement and nervousness, and gathered all the necessary paperwork to begin her first semester. Martina had always been an excellent student, and though it pained her to think of the years lost, she couldn't help but feel a glimmer of hope for the future. She regretted not attending college sooner, but now, she was taking control of her life—starting fresh, one step at a time.

Several hours later, Martina returned to her parents' house, her heart still racing from the whirlwind of the day. As she pulled into the driveway, she spotted her soon-to-be-ex-husband standing there, seething with anger. Without a word, she got out of the car and calmly told him, "I've just filed for divorce. I'm moving in with my parents. It's over."

His face twisted with rage. He shouted at her, but Martina stood firm, unshaken. Before things could escalate further, her father emerged from the house, rifle in hand, his presence as imposing as the weapon. Without a word, he leveled the rifle at the ground, a silent but clear warning. Her soon-to-be-ex hesitated, glared one last time, and then, realizing he was no match for her father, stormed off. That was the last time Martina ever saw him. Shortly after the divorce was finalized, he left Loving without a word and never returned.

The rest of the evening was spent in the warmth of her parents' home, surrounded by the laughter and chatter of family. She tucked the kids into bed, kissed them goodnight, and then, with a quiet nod to her mother, told her she was going for a run. Grabbing her father's flashlight, she slipped out into the cool night air, feeling a sense of freedom she hadn't known in years.

Martina ran—really ran—for the first time in a long while. She felt her body, once weighed down by aches and exhaustion, come alive with strength. Each stride was effortless, her legs carrying her faster than she had ever imagined. No more pain. No more fear. Just the pure joy of movement, of reclaiming herself.

She sprinted, fueled by something deep inside, and didn't stop until she reached the cave. She didn't hesitate at the entrance. The path was clear, no boulders blocking her way. She stepped forward into the dark, knowing that what awaited her inside would mark the beginning of a new chapter in her life.

Turning on the flashlight, Martina made her way through the mouth of the cave and toward the lake area, her heart pounding with anticipation. There, waiting as if she had been expecting her, stood Lala.

"I was going to send my owl to find you since you hadn't shown up," Lala said with a slight smile, her voice warm but tinged with concern.

Martina paused, taking a breath. "I had a few things to take care of before I came… things I should have done the first time," she replied, her voice heavy with the weight of her decisions.

Lala nodded understandingly but didn't press further. "Did you ask your parents about the cave?" she inquired.

"No, not yet," Martina said, shaking her head. "There was too much to do today. I wanted to see you first. I need to understand everything—the dragon eggs, how you brought me back to 1988, my future... and my children's future. There's so much I don't know. You have a lot of explaining to do, dear great-grandmother."

As Martina spoke, she couldn't help but notice how little Lala had changed. The woman before her looked just as she had in 2027—no older, no younger, as though time had not touched her at all. A strange sense of unease washed over Martina, but she couldn't shake the feeling that there were answers here, answers she desperately needed.

Lala met Martina's gaze, her expression unreadable. "Yes, I will explain everything. But first, you must understand—there's little time to waste. You have much to do, Martina. Bring the children tomorrow. They must bond with the dragon eggs."

Martina stood frozen for a moment, taking in Lala's words. The weight of what was to come felt like a heavy cloak settling over her shoulders. She had no choice but to follow this strange, mysterious path. But first, Martina herself had to make sense of it all, to understand what it meant for her and her children.

"NO!" she hissed, her voice filled with disbelief. "It's too soon. They're still babies!"

Lala's gaze softened, her tone patient but firm. "Granddaughter, your children are already at the age when a rider bonds with their dragon. Bring them, and you will see."

Martina blinked in confusion. "What do you mean? They're only two and three."

Lala nodded as if this were nothing new. "The egg is usually placed in the child's crib at birth. The dragon within learns its rider's heartbeat, bonding with the child from the very beginning. The child is drawn to the egg naturally. It will hatch when the child is ready, regardless of age."

Martina stood frozen, her mind racing. "You want my children to have a living dragon with them? They're two and three years old. That's far too young. What if the dragon attacks them? What if it… eats my child?" The thought was unthinkable.

Lala's expression didn't waver. "The dragon will not harm them. It will bond with them and they will understand each other. The bond is sacred. It is the way of the dragon and rider."

Martina's stomach stirred with the weight of it all. "Not to mention… how can I expect them to keep something so enormous a secret from their family?"

"The dragon and rider bond is strong," Lala explained. "The children will understand. It is their responsibility to protect the secret until the time comes."

Martina felt the sharp edges of fear and uncertainty gnawing at her, but she knew there was no turning back. Lala's words held a truth that could not be ignored. Still, she needed time to digest it all.

"Now, go home and rest," Lala advised. "It's very late. Bring the children tomorrow, and I will explain more then."

Martina nodded, a sense of quiet resolve settling over her. She had so many questions, but they would have to wait. She turned and walked out of the cave, her feet carrying her back to her children. The cool night air kissed her skin as she jogged back, her mind swirling with a thousand thoughts. She returned to her parents' home, which was now her home again. She took a quick shower, then crawled into bed, her body and mind exhausted from the events of the day.

Martina slept deeply for the first time in years, her body exhausted but her mind restless. Shadows twisted in her dreams, whispers of ancient secrets, the gleam of dragon eyes watching her from the darkness. She saw the eggs pulsing with life and felt the heat of unseen flames licking at her skin. Then came the feeling of something vast and powerful stirring beneath her, a presence both awe-inspiring and terrifying.

A low growl echoed in her mind, vibrating through her bones. A dragon's breath, warm and thick, fanned across her face. It was calling her and calling her children.

She wanted to wake up. But she couldn't.

The visions held her captive, showing glimpses of a future she didn't yet understand, her children standing before enormous beasts, their small hands reaching out as wings unfurled, claws scraping against stone. And then, something darker, a flash of fire, a scream, the feeling of loss so sharp it stole her breath.

Martina jolted awake, gasping, her heart hammering against her ribs. For a moment, she couldn't tell where she was. The darkness of her childhood bedroom pressed in around her, suffocating, unfamiliar despite the comfort it should have offered.

Her skin was slick with sweat. Her hands trembled as she pushed the blankets away.

She had wanted answers. Now, she wasn't sure she could handle them.

As she sat there, struggling to steady her breathing, one thing became terrifyingly clear—her life had changed forever, and there was no going back.

CHAPTER TEN

The next day, Martina drove to the caves. She was not walking there with a two-year-old and a three-year-old in tow. The children were eighteen months apart, and while they were full of energy, she worried about what they were about to encounter—Lala, the dragon eggs, and whatever destiny was unfolding before them.

She parked near the ditch, unbuckled the kids, and took their small hands in hers. The walk to the cave was short, but Martina's heart pounded with every step, especially after the nightmare she had that night. Was she really about to introduce her toddlers to something as dangerous, no, as impossible… as dragons?

Lala was waiting just inside the cave entrance, her wild gray hair and tattered robes making her look like an ancient ghost. But Angelica and Christopher weren't afraid. To Martina's surprise, they took to Lala instantly, as if they had always known her.

Lala led them deeper into the cave, where the air grew thick with heat. Martina swallowed hard when they entered what Lala called the nesting room. The glow of molten lava reflected off the cavern walls, casting eerie shadows. At the center of it all sat the nest … massive, lined with smooth black stones, and cradling several dragon eggs.

Angelica wasted no time. She let go of Martina's hand and approached the nest, circling it with the curiosity of a child drawn to something that had always belonged to her. Then, she stopped in front of a sapphire-blue egg, its surface shimmering like the ocean under sunlight.

Martina's stomach clenched. "Angelica, don't—" She rushed forward, ready to snatch her daughter away from the burning heat of the lava stones.

"Leave her," Lala said calmly, her voice echoing with a mysterious authority. "She will not get burned; this is her destiny."

Martina hesitated, torn between a burning fear and a baffling trust that Lala's words demanded. At that moment, Angelica, almost as if guided by an unseen force, placed both hands on the smooth surface of the sapphire egg.

When her tiny fingers made contact, the egg trembled and wobbled in a slumberous beat. Suddenly, Angelica's head flew back and her eyes turned an eerie, milky white as if she were peering into another realm. Panicked, Martina lunged forward, desperately grabbing her daughter. "What's happening to her? Lala, help her!" she cried, her voice shaky with terror.

Lala's expression softened as she spoke, almost whispering through the thick air, "Leave her be, Martina. She is having a premonition, a glimpse of what lies ahead."

In an instant, as if a spell had been lifted, Angelica's eyes returned to their normal, sparkling state. Slowly, she turned to Martina, her voice calm and filled with certainty. "Mama… Mine! My egg!"

A shiver ran down Martina's spine as she stared at her daughter, now glowing with a strange inner light. The cave's shadows seemed to lean in closer and the low hum filled the space between them, leaving Martina to wonder what destiny awaited her child.

"Are you okay, Mija? What happened to you? What did you see?" Martina asked.

"My dragon, I was flying on my blue dragon." Angelica giggled.

Martina's breath caught in her throat. *This is real. This is happening.* She turned to Lala, panic rising in her chest. "Is she…? I mean, is the bond already forming?"

Lala simply nodded, her expression unreadable.

Martina's heart pounded as she turned back to her daughter. Angelica tenderly caressed the egg, pressing tiny kisses against its smooth surface like holding a precious treasure.

"Mama, look! My blue egg!" Angelica beamed, blissfully unaware of the storm of emotion roiling within Martina.

Lala knelt beside the child, her voice both soft and commanding. "You must love your dragon with all your heart, speak to him daily, and protect him with your life."

Martina's stomach churned at the implication. "Lala, she's only three years old," she protested, her voice trembling with disbelief and dread. "Protecting him with her life—that's a bit extreme, don't you think?"

Lala's dark and knowing gaze met Martina's with a power that sent a chill down her spine, even amid the cave's burning heat. "You do not yet understand," Lala intoned quietly. "But you will."

A shiver raced along Martina's skin. She had come seeking answers yet found herself entangled in something far more significant and dangerous than she could have imagined.

Martina rolled her eyes and kneeled next to Angelica. "Girlie girl, this will be your dragon, and when the time comes, you will know what to do, okay?"

Angelica smiled at Martina and Lala, embraced and kissed her dragon egg again, and said "good dragon".

Christopher wriggled free from Martina's arms and crawled with curious determination toward the nest of eggs. He stood beside the nest, slowly circling its edge as if drawn by an invisible force. When he stopped in front of a vivid crimson egg, he reached out and touched it. To his surprise, the egg shuddered in response.

At that moment, the same mysterious shift that had overtaken Angelica gripped Christopher. His head sprang back and his eyes turned a frightening snow-white, an unmistakable sign that he, too, was experiencing an intense premonition. His eyes gradually returned to their natural deep-brown as if a spell were breaking. He turned to Martina and flashed a gentle, knowing smile, a silent confirmation that he had already met his dragon, even at just eighteen months old.

Christopher's egg was nearly as large as he was, a weighty promise of destiny. With all the determination a toddler could muster, he tried to lift the egg from the nest, but it proved too heavy for his little arms. Sensing his struggle, Martina quickly stepped forward and helped him, carefully lifting the egg and placing it on the ground in front of him.

Christopher sank down, nestling the egg between his legs and resting his head on its smooth surface as if seeking comfort in its warmth. Both children had imprinted with their dragon eggs during their first visit to that enchanted space. Imitating Angelica's earlier words, Christopher attempted to speak, his small voice filled with wonder: "My dagon."

Angelica leaned over with a playful correction, "Not 'Dagon', Brother, it's 'Dragon'."

Martina smiled, watching their playful exchange but in the flickering shadows of the cave, amid the soft glow of mysterious light, she watched her children with a mix of awe and fear. Their innocent actions revealed a destiny intertwined with dragons, ancient secrets, and a future that would forever change their lives.

"Now what?" Martina asked, her voice laced with uncertainty.

"Now we wait for the eggs to hatch," Lala replied, her gaze fixed on the shaded mouth of the cave. "Bring the children as often as possible. If you can, find a place nearby. They need to be with their dragons daily."

Martina sighed, shaking her head. "Lala, I told you, I can't just move here. My father would never give me this property near the caves; it's pastureland for the cattle. I'll have to stay with my parents until I can afford to build, and that won't be for a long time."

Lala's eyes darkened. "Your grandfather Ben had different plans." She paused, letting the words sink in before continuing. "Many years before your birth, he opened a savings account in your name. He deposited more than enough money for you to build a home, support the children, and so much more."

Martina blinked, stunned. "What? That's—"

"And that's not all," Lala interrupted. "Ben left you twenty acres of land, the very land surrounding these caves. He wanted you here, Martina. You can build your home right at the cave's entrance and begin the children's training immediately."

A chill ran down Martina's spine. She glanced back at the yawning cave, shadows curling at its entrance as if they were listening. "Why didn't anyone tell me?" she whispered.

"There are things your father does not know," Lala said cryptically. "Things even you are not ready to understand."

Martina's thoughts swirled. Her grandfather's generosity was overwhelming, almost surreal. The money, the land, everything had been prepared for her before she was even born. A plan set in motion long ago.

She swallowed hard. "This is… a lot."

"There will be many expenses," Lala continued, her voice gentle but firm. "This money will support your everyday life, cover your college, and ensure that Angelica and Christopher receive the training they need. But, Martina, listen to me." She stepped closer, lowering her voice. "This path is not without sacrifice. There is much more you need to know, but for now, return home. Speak with your parents about me… about the cave. Prepare yourself, Martina. There is no turning back."

A shiver prickled Martina's skin. The way Lala said it, as if some unseen forces were already moving, already shifting the course of her life, sent a wave of alarm through her. She nodded slowly. "I'll talk to them." But deep down, she knew something had already begun.

As Martina drove back to her parents' home, a whirlwind of thoughts stirred in her mind. *I must be losing it.* Encouraging her children to bond with dragon eggs? That was supposed to be normal? And now she was meant to build a home—their home—right next to a dragon lair? She let out a dry laugh. *Sure. That's perfectly fine. Nothing strange about that at all.*

Shaking her head, she tried to push away the overwhelming reality pressing in on her. But one thought refused to fade: "This path is not without sacrifices. There's no turning back."

Lala's words echoed in her mind, laced with something heavy, something unspoken. But what kind of sacrifices? What had she just agreed to? Martina tightened her grip on the steering wheel. Lala was so cryptic… *but why do I feel like I've already stepped over a line I can't see?*

Angelica's voice pulled Martina from the storm of her thoughts. "Mommy, I miss my dragon. I want to sleep in the cave with her, brother, brother's dragon, and you and Lala."

"Dagon!" Christopher chimed in excitedly, his little voice full of determination.

Martina exhaled … her children's words sealing her decision. There was no more room for doubt. She would tell her parents that her new home would be built on the twenty acres near the caves. But the thought of breaking the news to her father weighed on her. He had always seen that land as pasture for the cattle. How would he take it, knowing he was losing those acres?

He would, in fact, lose that land since Martina planned to enclose the entire area, shielding it from prying eyes. There could be no risk, no unwanted attention.

For a fleeting moment, doubt crept in, whispering that she was walking into the unknown and giving up too much. But she silenced it. Shaking off the uncertainty, Martina steadied herself. She had to follow her destiny.

CHAPTER ELEVEN

As soon as she arrived home, Martina wasted no time. She grabbed her purse, loaded the kids into the car, and drove straight to the bank in the nearby city of Carlsbad. Her heart pounded with anticipation as she stepped inside, unable to contain the emotions rushing through her. Sitting across from the bank teller, she handed over her ID, her palms slightly damp. The moment the teller pulled up the account details, Martina felt her breath hitch.

Her jaw dropped. *This can't be right.*

Her fingers trembled as she scanned the numbers on the screen. She and the kids were not only financially stable but also millionaires. A stunned laugh escaped her lips. She had expected a comfortable sum, enough to get by and build a modest home. But this?

This changed everything.

There was more than enough to build a house, a real home, near the caves. Enough to send the children to the best schools, pay for their training, secure their future, and still have plenty left.

She leaned back in her chair, exhaling slowly. *Grandpa Ben, what did you know? What were you preparing me for?*

A sense of awe, gratitude, and something else, something more profound, settled over her. The money and the land weren't just an inheritance—they were a responsibility. And ready or not, her new life had already begun.

When Martina returned to her parents' house, she wasted no time. She picked up the phone and called Legacy Home Builders, contracting them to begin construction on her new home immediately. To her relief, they agreed to come out the following day to discuss plans.

With that settled, Martina loaded the kids into the car and headed to the farm. She spotted her father atop his tractor, tilling the land. Her pulse quickened as she pulled up beside him. "Please, Goel," she prayed silently. "Let him understand."

Her father noticed her car and stopped the tractor, climbing down and dusting off his hands as he approached. "How'd your trip to Carlsbad go?" he asked, his sharp gaze scanning her face. "Are you able to talk about what's going on with you?"

Martina swallowed the lump in her throat and took a deep breath. "Dad… there's something I need to tell you."

She didn't hold back. She told him everything, the caves, the dragons, her encounter with Lala, and the impossible truth that she had been sent back in time to set things right.

Her father's expression shifted from curiosity to surprise to something unreadable. He studied her for a long moment, and Martina braced herself for disbelief and for anger over the land. But when he finally spoke, his voice was calm. "I always knew the land was yours."

Martina blinked. "What?"

"Your grandfather made sure of it. But when you moved to Loving and didn't have plans to live on the farm, I figured there was no reason to bring it up. I've been using it for the cattle until you were ready."

Shock rippled through Martina. He had known all along. A weight she hadn't realized she was carrying lifted from her shoulders. She had been preparing for an argument, but instead, her father had simply been waiting for her to be ready. And now, she was. "Dad, I wish you had told me. About the land, about the millions of dollars Papa Ben left me… and that I was destined to be the guardian of my children's dragon eggs."

Martina watched as her steady, no-nonsense father gave her a look of pure disbelief. His brows furrowed, his jaw tightening as if he were trying to make sense of something impossible.

"What do you mean my father left you millions of dollars? From where? And what do you mean by a guardian of dragon eggs?"

She took a deep breath, steadying herself. "Dad, Papa Ben set up a savings account for me before I was even born. I checked it today and there are millions in there. Enough to build a home, to provide for the kids, to make sure they're trained properly. A contractor is coming tomorrow afternoon to go over the plans."

Her father shook his head, stunned. "Martina… I had no idea about the savings account. That money could have helped raise all of you kids."

Martina placed a hand on his arm, grounding both him and herself. "No, Dad, you don't understand. This money wasn't meant for that, it was meant for me and the kids, for our future. Papa Ben knew this day would come. He knew I would have to raise my children as dragon riders." She softened her voice. "But of course, I'll help you with any expenses you have; there's plenty of money."

Her father ran a hand through his hair, exhaling sharply. He looked past her, out toward the horizon where the land stretched endlessly as if searching for answers in the wind.

"Dragon riders…?" he murmured, almost to himself.

Martina could see the struggle in his eyes, the part of him that wanted to reject it, to hold onto the quiet simplicity of their ranching life. But there was something else, something deeper. A knowing. The part of him that had never spoken of the land being hers, the part that had accepted the truth long before she had… That part of him already knew about the prophecy.

GM climbed into the car with Martina and the kids, a sense of determination settling over him. He knew he had to tell Isa the truth, that the prophecy was real, and that Martina, with the help of Lala, had uncovered it. The time for secrets was over. He turned and looked at Martina and the kids. "Let's go talk to your mother; she needs to hear the rest as much as I do."

When they arrived home, Isa was busy cooking lunch in the kitchen, her back to them as the aroma of simmering food filled the air. GM walked in first, followed by Martina and the children, and then Martina spoke with a gravity that silenced the room.

"Mom, we need to talk about the prophecy, the caves, and the dragons."

Isa whirled around, her face tightening with concern and anger. Her hands trembled as she gripped the counter's edge, her knuckles turning white.

"Hija, are you telling me you've been to that place?" Her voice wavered between fury and fear. "Since you were young, I warned you children never to go near those caves! Please, don't return there! There is great evil in that place."

She took a shaky breath before continuing, her voice thick with emotion. "When you were young, your brother went into those caves. He saw a witch, and she tried to kill him. He has never been the same since. She cursed him, Martina. The witch cursed him." Isa's eyes searched her daughter's face, pleading for understanding, for obedience … for fear.

Martina's heart sank, but she stood her ground.

"Mom, that wasn't a witch, it was Mama Lala. She's the current guardian of the Derdjanian dragons. She never tried to kill him. Scare him out of there maybe, but not kill. She's tattered, but she's perfectly sane and a believer in Goel."

Isa's face twisted with disbelief, and she shook her head, refusing to accept Martina's words. The past was too painful for her to let go of.

When Martina was young, GM had tried to tell Isa about the caves and their daughter's destiny to become the guardian. But Isa had been adamant, forbidding him ever to tell Martina about them. That was when Isa had demanded GM seal the caves, ensuring that none of the children could go near it.

What they didn't know, what they couldn't know, was the true purpose of the caves. They had no idea about the dragons, the coming devastation, or the war that loomed. Lala had told Martina that she could share all of it with her parents, but Martina had hesitated.

As she began to tell Isa and GM about Lala, the dragons, and her return from the future, Isa's face grew pale, her hands trembling as the weight of Martina's words sank in. She made the sign of the cross over herself, then said, "I... I need to sit down," her voice empty.

GM stepped closer, attempting to calm her, but the story was beyond their understanding. The weight of the truth, of the things they hadn't wanted to know, was too much. GM turned to Martina, his voice filled with regret. "I'm sorry I kept such a secret from you all these years. I didn't believe in the prophecy or know about dragons or the money your grandfather left you."

He paused, and then, with a fierce resolve, added, "But if I'm going to give up one of my daughters to become a guardian of dragon eggs and live in a cave for the rest of her life, I should be able to see what you're getting yourself into."

Martina considered his words carefully. The depth of her father's concern wasn't lost on her. He had always been protective of the family, and now, more than ever, he needed to understand. "Yes, I think it's time for both of you to see the caves and Lala."

CHAPTER TWELVE

A few days later, Martina and GM drove down to the caves. Construction had already started on Martina's new house. The contractor had come, and within a few days, they had equipment and men working to clear the area. The concrete foundation would be poured in a few days; in the meantime, the plumbing was being placed. Her two-story house would be over 4,000 square feet. It would be her dream home and was going to be amazing. The home would be large enough to practice training indoors, depending on the weather. The contractors probably thought she was crazy, but no matter what, Martina knew what had to be done.

"Why do you need such a big house? It's just you and the kids."

"Dad, I already explained that my family will soon be growing. Plus, if you and Mom ever want to move in with us, there will be plenty of space. Dad, the war is several years away, but it will be here one day; we must be prepared."

GM considered Martina's statement. "Okay, but I don't think I can convince your mother to come live here. Your mother didn't want to come today; she's afraid for you and the children. She has always believed these caves are a curse, she believes demonic forces are working against us."

"Dad, Goel is with us; he is our creator and our redeemer. We must do our part in the war to come and Goel will save us all." Martina prayed to herself, she hoped GM would believe her and that he would be able to convince Isa and the rest of the family. Her father was considered the patriarch of the Basquez family. He was the eldest son and had never shown favoritism toward his siblings or his children. GM was truly a testament to his unwavering sense of fairness and leadership. His decisions were always guided by wisdom, compassion, and a deep sense of responsibility, which earned him the respect and admiration of all who knew him.

"Come on, Dad, let's go see Mama Lala."

Martina drove around the back side of the caves. The main entrance was hidden, and she didn't want one of the contractors to stumble in by accident. Too many secrets lay within. GM stepped out of the truck, eyeing the dark, jagged mouth of the cave with suspicion. "What's the matter, Dad? Did you change your mind?"

"No," he said slowly, "but I have a question. Do you think Lala or the dragons will try to kill me?"

Martina snorted. "What? No, Dad, no one's going to try to hurt you. Besides, Lala is too old, you could take her on! And the dragons?" A smirk tugged at her lips. "They haven't hatched yet."

GM wasn't convinced. "Right," he muttered, shaking his head. "Okay, let's do this."

The entrance was a tight squeeze for GM. They would definitely need to widen it, make it larger, and conceal it far better. There was no telling who might come snooping.

As they stepped inside, the cavern's overpowering darkness swallowed them whole. Martina flicked on her flashlight and handed her father one. The beam slicing through the blackness revealed jagged rock formations that loomed like crooked teeth.

GM scanned the space warily, noting the cracked, crumbling stone. "This place is a death trap," he muttered.

The air was thick, damp, and laced with an acrid, almost rotten scent that made his nose wrinkle. The steady hum of unseen insects whispered through the cavern, blending with an underground waterfall's low, guttural murmur. It was a soothing yet menacing sound, like a distant predator waiting to strike.

A shiver crept up GM's spine. He wasn't sure if it was the cold—or the feeling that something was watching them from the depths.

Martina breathed deeply, feeling the cave awaken something primal inside her. She loved this place.

Then … A scream. Not a normal scream.

It was jagged and warped, like something was choking on its own agony. The sound slithered through the tunnels, echoing endlessly. Martina's skin prickled. GM stiffened.

"What was that?" His voice was tight. "Is this normal?"

"No." Her heartbeat hammered in her ears. "Something's wrong. Get behind me."

She reached under her shirt and pulled out a gun. GM gaped at her. "Where the heck did you get that?"

"Dad, that's not important." Her voice was low, sharp. Her eyes gleamed in the dim light. Martina tightened her grip on the gun.

They pressed on, the eerie scream now replaced by an unsettling silence. As they reached the lake, she turned to her father, who stood frozen, his eyes wide with awe as he took in the sheer enormity of the cave. The expression on his face was priceless. "Dad, are you okay? Do you need to sit down?" she asked.

"I can't believe this has been here all these years," he murmured. "I've lived here my whole life and never knew this existed. It's… beautiful."

Martina smiled. "That's exactly what I thought when I first came here. There's so much more; I can't wait for you to see it and the dragon eggs, but first, let's find out where that scream came from."

Martina spotted Lala on the far side of the lake, standing over a kneeling figure. Without hesitation, she and GM took off, racing around the water's edge until they reached her.

Lala's lips moved in a hushed, rhythmic murmur; was she chanting? The kneeling man before her convulsed violently, his body seizing as if caught between two worlds. Martina's pulse pounded in her ears.

"What are you doing? Who is this?" she demanded, her voice tight with unease.

Lala didn't respond. Her eyes, now a chilling, unnatural white, locked onto Martina, sending a cold shiver clawing up her spine. The air in the cave thickened, pressing down like an unseen force. Was Lala harming him? Cursing him?

Then, with a sudden jolt, the man stopped shaking. His head snapped up, his expression eerily vacant. He rose unnaturally and walked without a word toward the cave's shadowed exit.

"Lala," Martina whispered, dread curling in her gut, "what's going on?"

Lala turned her head slowly, her white eyes narrowing. And then, she smiled.

Lala snapped out of her trance and looked up at Martina, then at GM. She took a deep breath as if grounding herself, before breaking into her brightest smile. "*Nieto, como estas?*" she asked. As if nothing had happened. "Abuela, is that you?"

GM believed his grandmother had passed away years before. He never imagined Lala living in a cave; it was impossible. How was she still alive after all these years? Lala came close to GM and placed her hands on his arms. There was always a certain amount of disconnect with Lala, but Martina knew she cared enough to guard the eggs and protect their integrity at all costs. Martina's voice rang out, sharp with urgency, "Who was that man; what did you do to him? Did he see the dragon eggs?"

Lala turned to her, unfazed. "He wandered in by accident," she said calmly. "My owl warned me that he had reached the lake, so I simply... persuaded him to leave and forget he ever found this place. Goel has blessed this old woman with gifts, just as He will bless you, granddaughter."

Martina had both her hands on the side of her head; she couldn't believe someone had discovered the cave. Not to mention make it to the lake, or worse, discover the dragon eggs. "We need to secure the cave entrance so this doesn't ever happen again," said Martina.

"Don't worry, Martina," Lala reassured her. "This isn't the first time someone has found their way here. Your brother, Lukas, was the first. Then your sisters, Willow and Marguerite, came too. I gently persuaded them to forget they'd ever been here."

"What?" Martina's voice rose in disbelief. "My sisters were here! When?"

Lala chuckled. "They were very young when they wandered in. They were going for a swim in the lake, much like you and your cousin wanted to when you first visited the caves all those years ago."

"This can never happen again," Martina said firmly. "We need to secure the entrance. Dad, can you come up with something so only we can access it?"

GM furrowed his brow, thinking hard, then nodded. "Absolutely. I'll figure something out as soon as we get to the house."

Satisfied, Martina turned to Lala, her voice softening with gratitude. "Thank you for protecting the dragon eggs, grandmother."

Martina and her grandmother walked through the caves with GM. He was amazed at the massive size of the caverns. "Can anyone swim in the lake or bathe if needed?" GM gave Lala a quizzical look.

"Dad, just come out and ask Lala if this is where she bathes!" Martina laughed out loud at the thought of Lala with her bath towel and bar of soap in the cold water. She wanted to tell her dad that, by the look of Lala, she hadn't bathed in years. But she didn't go that far as to insult her great-grandmother.

"Nieto, I have a small pond in a separate cave heated by the same coals that keep the nest warm. Goel has allowed me and the eggs to stay warm on cold days. Otherwise, the cave temperature stays the same all year round." They continued walking around the separate caves, and Lala showed them where she slept and ate.

"Grandson, how have you been since I last saw you? Look how thin you are. Is your wife not feeding you? Your father was always plump; you didn't take after him. How is your family, your mother, and your sister?" Lala asked, her voice filled with warmth. "I loved your sister so much," Lala continued, her words flowing for what felt like a lifetime, reminiscing about the past, each story blending into the next.

After a long visit, she invited GM to the nesting room. The room glowed from the hot coals; the aroma in the cave was musky yet floral—it was captivating. GM guardedly approached the nest; he couldn't believe his eyes. Martina hesitantly stepped towards her father. She put one hand on his arm and said, "Dad, meet the Derdjanian dragons; I will guard them and protect them with my life. Come closer, Dad, and feel their strength and their power."

Seeing the enormous nest full of colorful dragon eggs was unbearable for GM. He went down on his knees and prayed; GM implored Goel for mercy and understanding. Martina's father reached out for her hand and thanked her. "Martina, you have completed this impossible task yet remained confident and courageous. How can I help?"

Martina looked into her father's face, tears welling in her eyes. "Dad, you must keep this secret to yourself; not a word of this must ever leave your lips to another soul. The threat of exposure is too great."

GM understood and swore never to speak of it and assured Martina that he would take this secret to his grave.

"Can I touch one?" GM asked.

"Do you feel as though the egg is calling to you, pulling at your chest?" asked Lala.

"No, I just want to touch one."

Lala said, "Grandson, you will get burned if you touch a dragon egg without being called. Only a dragon rider and the guardian can handle the eggs, no one else."

GM raised his hands in surrender and stepped away. The calling had not been for him. Martina and her father said goodbyes and headed back to the house.

CHAPTER THIRTEEN

Her mother stood in the garden with Angelica and Christopher, the late-afternoon sun casting long shadows across the grass. As soon as she spotted Martina, her face paled. Without a word, she turned and walked inside, her retreat swift, almost desperate.

Martina's chest tightened. The fear in Isa's eyes was more than she could bear. She exhaled shakily, swallowing the sting of rejection. She wanted, no, she needed, a real relationship with her mother. She wouldn't let anything stand in the way, no matter what it took.

"Don't worry about your mother," GM murmured, watching the house with knowing eyes. "She'll come around... one day."

But Martina wasn't so sure. Isa never spoke of the visit, questioned it, or acknowledged its existence. It was as if, in her mind, it had never happened. And somehow, that was more unsettling than if she had.

GM returned to the cave daily to visit Lala and to check on the eggs. He had built a small building around the cave, which concealed the entrance. There was a sturdy lock on the door, and only he and Martina had the key; this would keep anyone else from wandering in. GM took Angelica and Christopher to see their dragon eggs when Martina was in college; the kids loved to spend time with their grandfather, especially when it meant they could go to the caves for a visit.

On one of their outings, Christopher tried handing the egg to GM. Lala would give him the look—threatening, devious, yet protected. Angelica would squint her eyes at Lala and pout her lips. She did not like Lala making faces at her grandpa.

Martina went to college every day and was determined to get a degree. She was well aware of the coming expenses, so she decided to dip into her grandfather's savings and invest in the stock market. Though she believed she had made solid choices with reputable funds, every bit of income was crucial to turning her plans into reality.

As the months passed, Martina mended her relationship with her cousin; she had missed Anna in her previous life and wasn't about to let anything ruin the friendship. Martina told Anna she had returned to the cave years before and that there was nothing there. "Why hadn't you told me before this? I've been so afraid to come near your house, Martina."

"Anna, you wouldn't speak to me through most of our high school years, then you married and moved off. The cave is amazing! Hopefully, you can come back there with me," suggested Martina.

Anna gave Martina a worried glance, then said, "No, I think I'll take your word for it and steer clear of the cave for now!"

"You know I'm building my new house there? My dad gave me some land, and I wanted the caves in my backyard so the kids and I can go for a swim everyday if we wanted to."

"Why would you want to go there every day? That cave is so creepy and dangerous!"

Martina decided not to push the subject of the cave any further, so she laughed and hugged her cousin. "You are my best friend, I never want us to go a day without speaking again, which should last for the rest of our lives."

"You got it, Cuz!"

Anna and Martina were closer than ever; she had her best friend back.

Even though Anna moved to Las Cruces after her divorce, they remained close. Martina had always hoped to share her story about the dragons with Anna someday, but it was clear that the moment for that was not now. For the time being, she would have to accept that having Anna back in her life, even without those secrets being shared, was enough.

CHAPTER FOURTEEN

Martina and her children's new home was ready to move into—the excitement was unbearable. She was glad her parents had accepted them into their home for the past year and a half, but it was time to be on their own. Well, at least until Marcus came into their lives in a few years. "Mama, can we have a big party and invite everyone to our new home?" asked Angelica.

"Of course, let's make it the best party ever!"

The house was incredible; the architect had done an amazing job with the layout. The home's exterior had a wraparound porch around the house, with areas enclosed for cold winter days. Inside, the open-concept floor plan had been a great idea; once one entered the grand double doors, the enormous living room flowed into the kitchen and dining area. There were three separate sitting areas in various locations for the "I want to be cozy and read a book day." The sliding glass doors opened into the back patio and swimming pool/ hot tub area. Martina hadn't wanted trees too close to the patio area since those nasty doves would perch on the trees and poop everywhere. Yuck!

An oversized waterproof sunshade sail canopy shaded the entire backyard. A steel-framed staircase led to the five bedrooms, library, study room, and another family room. Each bedroom had its bathroom; this was a necessity. Martina had never imagined in her wildest dreams that she would own such an extravagant home—she was elated.

Angelica and Christopher were ecstatic because the caves were now part of their backyard. They were far enough away from the house that no one would venture too close to them, yet close enough that the kids could walk. The shed that concealed the cave entrance blended in with the landscaping and looked quite picturesque. Lala gave Martina the idea to plant live oak trees around the shed and build a playhouse for the kids in the same area; it was the perfect cover-up. Martina wanted the kids to be able to visit their dragons any time of the day, and she would be close by if needed.

Martina also enclosed the entirety of her property with a fifteen-foot steel wall for privacy; it looked like a fortress. They would need to be as secluded as possible once the dragons hatched; there could be no prying eyes. Besides, even in her previous life, Martina had always been a recluse; she didn't care about outside influences. She believed in the *I'd call or text if I wanted you in my business* attitude.

The days for cell phones at your fingertips were soon to come. That would be extremely handy about now. She claimed to be concerned about someone breaking in or keeping out coyotes or any other wild animals in the area. Martina told her family she was a mile from GM's house and worried about their safety.

Her siblings just laughed and said it was a good idea. Martina was pretty sure her sisters thought she was crazy.

It had to be this way; she had to protect Angelica and Christopher, the dragon eggs, and the cave!

Martina invited all her siblings and parents for a big gathering the following weekend. Excited by the idea, she declared it a housewarming party, suggesting everyone bring a dish to share.

Determined to have all her loved ones together, Martina called Anna, practically begging her to come. After a long pause, Anna hesitantly agreed. She arrived the day before the party with her son, Brian, ready to spend the weekend with Martina and the kids.

The moment Anna stepped inside, her eyes darted toward the back glass doors. Her expression tightened. "Please tell me you bulldozed the caves. I don't want my son anywhere near them."

Martina forced a reassuring smile. "Don't worry, cousin. He'll be safe here. He can't get to the caves."

Anna exhaled, but Martina could see the tension still in her posture. She longed to tell Anna the truth, to share the secret she had kept for so long. But Anna wasn't ready. Not yet. Martina silently prayed to Goel that her cousin would understand one day about the caves, the dragons, and the duty she bore. Keeping this from her best friend was the hardest thing of all.

The following day, the house buzzed with laughter and conversation as family and friends gathered for the party. It was a resounding success. The food was plentiful and the atmosphere was warm and lively. But amidst the celebration, a quiet vigilance remained. Christopher's and Angelica's ability to keep the secret of the dragon eggs was unmatched, making them the perfect protectors of something so rare and powerful.

Martina glanced toward the caves as the festivities continued, her heart both heavy and hopeful. One day, the truth would come to light. But until then, the dragons remained a secret, one she would guard with everything she had.

CHAPTER FIFTEEN

When Angelica was six and a half and Christopher five, Martina purchased six quarter-horses and began teaching her children to ride. The colts and fillies, though young, were well-trained and the kids took to the saddle like they were born for it. Angelica, especially, had a fearless love for riding bareback, her laughter ringing through the fields as she galloped across the land.

One afternoon, Angelica tugged at her mother's sleeve, her eyes bright with determination. "Mama, can I ride to Grandpa's house on my horse? He's an old man, and I don't want him getting tired driving over here."

Martina chuckled. "Angelica, Grandpa is only sixty-two. That's not old."

"Yes, he is!" Angelica insisted, crossing her arms. "Grandpa said, 'Don't jump on my back because I'm an old man."

Martina sighed, shaking her head with a smirk. "Aye, ya, yay, there is no winning this argument. Alright, girlie girl, get your brother," she said with a grin, grabbing her hat. "Let's saddle up and ride to Grandpa's house."

Christopher ran to his horse and expertly secured the harness all by himself. Martina watched in awe, a swell of pride filling her chest. *Fantastic*, she thought. *My kids are amazing!* Not only had they mastered horseback riding, but their grandpa had already taught them to drive go-karts and introduced them to the ins and outs of farming. With her natural green thumb and the help of her grandpa, Angelica began planting crops as if she had been born to work the land. They had planted a garden with vegetables and herbs in Martina's backyard. Meanwhile, barely five years old, Christopher learned to ride his bicycle and fix his flat tires. After all, they lived on a farm and bicycle tires went flat easily.

With the help of her sister, Lena, and her husband, Martina had also taught the kids essential survival skills. They had learned to hunt, fish, and shoot a bow and arrow, skills that would serve them well for years. Watching them grow into capable and independent children filled Martina with pride and gratitude.

Martina shuddered as she recalled her first life—how easily she had fallen into the trap of convenience, feeding her children whatever was quick and easy, drowning them in processed foods and sugary drinks. She had been too consumed by work, too exhausted to care, until it was too late. The weight of regret pressed down on her chest like a vice. She had watched sickness creep into her home, lurking in every careless meal and skipped moments of care.

This time, she would not let them down. No more laziness. Martina and her children would be strong and resilient, untouched by the fate that had once swallowed them whole.

Daily walks with her mother became a pleasant tradition, growing into a joyful way to welcome life's moments together. It was a little act of bravery against the march of time, especially after experiencing loss that felt too early. Angelica and Christopher often strolled alongside Isa, their small hands in hers, filling the air with laughter and sweet reminders of the bright future Martina promised to hold onto.

Whenever they could, her sisters and little brother joined too, their expanding families adding to the cheerful rhythm of their steps. Through it all, Martina focused on cherishing her time with her mother. Their bond had strengthened over the past few years, and Martina was determined never to lose that again.

She approached cooking with joy, putting care into every meal as if it were a shield against the illnesses that had affected her family in the past. No diabetes. No digestive issues. No gradual decline. She was determined to break the cycle and create a brighter future. This time, her family wouldn't just get by—they would truly flourish together!

The day Angelica turned seven, Martina and the children went to the caves to see their dragon eggs, which was their daily routine. Angelica cradled the egg as she always did when they visited. The air felt different in the cave today; hope was in the air. Martina watched the kids; they seemed unusually anxious and excited. "Mommy, my dragon says she will come out and see me today; she's ready to come out of the egg."

"Okay, we'll see what happens," said Martina.

"Mommy, my dragon too will come out today," said Christopher.

Martina looked at her children and wondered if they knew something she didn't. After all, they did have a bond with the dragons that she didn't understand. Martina spoke with Lala about what her next plans for the land were going to be and about the kids' training.

Suddenly, Angelica screamed, "Mommy, hurry, come here!"

Martina raced across the room in a second. "What happened? What's the matter?"

"Look, Mama!" The egg wiggled in Angelica's arms and began to glow, then there was a sudden loud crack—the egg was about to hatch. At that moment, the egg split in half, and out came a slimy, wet, sapphire dragon. Angelica was ecstatic. As she picked at the remainder of the shell, helping her dragon out, Angelica announced that Qadira was her dragon's name because she would be full of power.

Qadira was exquisite: her sapphire scales shone brightly and shimmered as she moved around. Angelica whispered to the dragon, a phrase that Martina didn't understand. "Angelica, what are you saying? What language did you speak?"

"Mama, I'm speaking to Qadira; she speaks Derdjanian."

Martina was amazed; she glanced over at Lala and gave her a questioning look. Lala smiled and nodded. Angelica continued to speak to her dragon in that beautiful language. Qadira looked around the cavern and then back at Angelica; she squealed and purred. Angelica set her down on the ground and everyone watched as Qadira attempted her first steps. Stumbling around Angelica, Qadira walked toward Christopher. Qadira nudged at his arm, and he petted Qadira and spoke Derdjanian to her.

What the heck? He knew how to speak the dragon's language? These kids were incredible!

Qadira made her way back to Angelica, climbed on her lap, and went right to sleep. Christopher held his dragon egg tightly, willing it to come out; he continued to caress it, then a wiggle, another wiggle, and a loud, thunderous crack! His crimson dragon emerged out of its encasing in one solid break down the center of the egg! He was magnificent, half the size of Christopher, and as it stretched out, its wingspan was twice its size.

Christopher hugged his dragon and quietly spoke in Derdjanian, comforting his new friend. The dragon nudged him under his chin; then they were nose to nose and eye to eye, bonding. After listening to the children communicating with their dragons for a while, Martina said, "I think I understand what they are saying."

"If it is the will of Goel, you will understand," replied Lala.

Martina couldn't believe it; she knew Derdjanian! "Christopher, what have you named your dragon?"

Christopher whispered to his dragon, then said, "My dragon's name is Ashraf because he is noble and honorable, but I will call him Blaze because he looks like a fireball." Everyone agreed that Christopher's dragon was formidable. Ashraf lay his giant head on Christopher's lap, thrummed, and fell asleep.

As Martina watched the children with their dragons, Lala slipped away toward the river, determined to catch fish for the young dragons' first meal. The air was thick with the scent of morning dew and something new—magical, perhaps. Martina's heart swelled with love and wonder; the long-awaited arrival of her children's dragons had finally come. She knew, deep down, that life would never be the same again.

Seated on the mossy ridge, Martina observed Christopher and Angelica bonding with their newfound companions. The dragons curled trustingly in their laps, scales shimmering softly in the light. But as Martina sat there, a strange sensation began to twist in her stomach. Was it fear? A faint anxiety about the uncertain road ahead? Or breakfast making its presence known? She chuckled to herself; parenthood had never come with a guidebook, and dragon-rearing wasn't in any of the chapters.

A flicker of doubt passed through her. She was allowing her children to cradle creatures that could devour them whole. Yet, despite the razor-sharp claws and fire-breathing potential, a surprising calm settled over her mind. Her heart held no panic, only a deep, echoing peace.

As she stood, stretching her legs, Martina felt something shift inside her. A gentle tug in her chest, insistent, almost aching. Her eyes drifted toward the large nest tucked beneath the ancient tree, cradling eggs the size of pumpkins. The pull grew stronger. Something was calling her, something waiting. With steady steps, she moved toward the nest, unaware that her story with the dragons was just beginning.

Martina walked around the nest and stopped before a sizable gold-colored egg. There was no doubt in her mind when she placed her hand on the egg—it pulsed under her touch. She quickly pulled away. Lala witnessed Martina's reaction as she entered the cave, prompting her to lay her hand on the egg again. She did as instructed, and there it was—the pulsing, throbbing, pounding feeling in her chest. She lifted the egg from the hot coals and instantly knew this was her dragon. She laid the egg down again and watched Lala through hot tears on her face.

Lala came closer. "Martina, you will be the guardian of the eggs. A dragon shouldn't be calling you, but as Goel wills it, this is happening. Pick up the dragon egg, granddaughter. Can you hear the call?"

Martina picked up the golden egg and felt it again, her heartbeat for the dragon within the egg. Tears poured down her face, tears of joy, of longing. She smiled and tried to speak, but no words came. Martina peered at Lala, who smiled and nodded with approval. She held the egg with large scales shimmering like polished brass. The roughness of each scale felt almost sharp to the touch. Martina whispered to her dragon quiet, comforting words, then laid one solid, long kiss on the egg, and a fissure appeared right at the spot where she had kissed.

Martina's dragon was hatching! She sat on the ground and set the egg on her lap as the golden dragon emerged from its shell. She immediately knew her dragon was a male through their bond. He peered at her through the broken surface, and she removed the shell pieces from his face and body. He was exquisite! The dragon's golden scales caught the light and sparkling diamonds danced throughout the cavern. His striking green eyes observed Martina lovingly. He purred, thrummed, then mentally spoke Derdjanian to her, and she understood every word!

Martina responded to her dragon, "Calme, Rachid, atokitamil." (Be calm, Rachid, I am with you.)

He responded with an "atokitamila". (I am also with you.)

Martina cupped Rachid's beautiful face in both hands, her thumbs brushing gently across his cheeks as she gazed into his deep, knowing eyes. At that moment, the world around her seemed to vanish; there was no running stream, no Rachid, and no breath. Time itself held still.

Then it hit her.

Martina's head snapped backward as though struck by lightning as a vision poured into her mind. Smoke billowed from burning cities, flames clawed at the sky. Screams echoed through the chaos as the nation rose against the nation. Famine carved hollows into once-healthy faces. Pestilence swept like a shadow, indiscriminate and cruel.

She saw winged and wailing dragons, riders atop them wielding light and fire, locked in brutal combat against monstrous forces twisted by darkness. The sky turned red with ash and fury. The ground was littered with the fallen—both beast and man.

Martina's breath caught in her throat. Though destruction reigned, Goel's presence burned like a beacon in the void, a promise that the darkness would not have the final word. He would lead them, guide them, and stand in the gap when all hope seemed lost.

And just as suddenly as it had come, the vision vanished. Martina gasped, her body folding inward, hands slipping from Rachid's face as she tried to stand, yet her legs were too weak. Tears streaked her cheeks and her chest heaved with the weight of what she'd seen.

She looked around, and Lala knelt beside her, Christopher and Angelica at her side. "Granddaughter, did you have a vision?"

Martina looked at Rachid; he had shared this vision with her. "How did you know?"

she asked Rachid. He snuggled in her arms and drifted off to sleep. "Lala, you were right; we must be prepared for what is to come; there is much to do."

"Mama, are you okay? What did Rachid show you?"

"I'm okay, Mija. Rachid showed me the future, and it's a little scary, but we will be ready for it, won't we?"

Both the kids and Lala nodded in agreement. "Ashraf is ready," said Christopher, "…and so is Qadira," chimed in Angelica. "Rachid will also be prepared when the time comes."

Martina looked down at her dragon, fast asleep in her lap. The vision she had seen made everything seem even more real. This was Goel's will, what must come, but they were far from ready.

CHAPTER SIXTEEN

Years passed, and Martina and the children continued training in ninjutsu, archery, karate, and other combative techniques. She wanted herself and the kids to be skilled warriors. Angelica and Christopher were young but never complained; they were dragon riders and proud of it. Martina and Lala spoke with the children about the future and the expectations of a dragon rider. There was no doubt in Martina's mind that she and the children were destined to be dragon riders.

Martina, Angelica, and Christopher attended a long-overdue family reunion the following day. The air buzzed with laughter, clinking glasses, and the warmth of reconnection. There, amid the hum of conversations and familiar faces, Martina first met her cousin, Samuel. This meeting would soon change everything. Within days, Samuel would introduce her to Marcus.

And Martina knew she had to get it right.

Everything had to unfold as it had before. When Martina first met Marcus, she'd fallen in love the instant their eyes had met, and that moment had been imprinted on her soul, unchanged by time and untouched by doubt. She couldn't risk a misstep now. The stakes were too high.

He had been the only man Martina had ever truly loved.

But fear crept in, quiet and cruel. What if something was different this time? What if he was different? What if he didn't feel the same attraction, spark, and unshakable connection she had felt? Could she bear the weight of rejection if he no longer looked at her as he once had? Would she survive loving him again if he didn't love her back?

No. She couldn't take that chance.

Martina followed every step she had once taken, the exact words, timing, and clothes even, desperate to preserve the thread of fate that had once brought them together. Every move was planned, every moment rehearsed. She prayed to Goel for nothing to go wrong. It had to be perfect. Because this wasn't just love, it was destiny, and Martina was walking a tightrope over everything she had ever wanted.

With time and prayer, their relationship flourished as if it was the first time. Martina and Marcus fell in love, and there was no doubt in her mind that they belonged together. Marcus had two daughters—Melanie, fifteen, and Kristie, seventeen—from a previous marriage he wanted to raise before his and Martina's relationship got too serious. All three would visit Martina, Angelica, and Christopher in Loving, yet Martina wasn't ready to show him their dragons. She was afraid to scare him off.

Months passed, and each day, Martina found herself loving Marcus even more deeply than she had in her previous life. Perhaps it was the mistakes she'd learned from, the wisdom hard-won through time and heartache. Or maybe it was simply that, this time, she cherished every moment with him as if it were borrowed from fate. Whatever the reason, she knew she was ready to share the truth about the dragons, the caves, and the future.

"Okay, kids," Martina said one crisp morning, her voice steady but her heart fluttering. "Today's the day we tell Marcus everything about our dragons, all of it."

Angelica's face was clouded with worry. "Mom… what if he gets scared? What if he thinks we're crazy and just leaves us? What if he never wants to see us again?"

Martina paused, kneeling so she could meet her daughter's eyes. "If that happens, Mija… then maybe he wasn't meant to be with us after all."

Angelica shook her head, tears brimming. "Don't say that, Mom. He is meant to be with us. I know it. He's going to love our dragons just like we do."

Martina smiled, pulling her daughter close. "I hope you're right, girlie girl. I really do. But no matter what happens, we'll face it together." She thought of the dragons snugly in the caves and prayed Marcus would feel the same way. But love, she believed, was more powerful than fear. It had to be.

Martina looked out at the front door; Marcus had arrived. She and the kids went out to greet him. "Hello there, this is a wonderful greeting."

Angelica and Christopher ran out and embraced him. Martina laughed and followed the kids' lead. They all sat out on the porch, Marcus watching them curiously. "Is everything all right? Why are you all looking at me that way?"

"We have something important to tell you," said Christopher.

"Keep an open mind," said Angelica.

Marcus peered through squinted eyes, his jaw tight. "The suspense is killing me. Let's hear it."

Martina took a deep breath, her fingers trembling. "Please… promise me you'll listen to everything before you say anything. No interruptions, okay?" He gave a slow nod, though unease crept into his features. "Where do I even start?" Her voice quivered. "Marcus… we knew each other before in another life. We were married for years. Then I found Lala." His brow furrowed, confusion flitting across his face, but he stayed silent.

Martina's voice dropped to a whisper as she recounted the memories burned into her soul—the owl in the cave, her mother's passing, and Lala. A cold shiver traced Marcus's spine, but he didn't speak.

"I was sent back in time, Marcus. I saw things no one should see. The dragon eggs were real and alive. Waiting. And then they hatched. For me.

For the children." Marcus didn't move. His face was unreadable. Still, his eyes searched hers like he was trying to decipher a language he'd never heard spoken aloud. Martina's heart hammered in her chest. She braced herself for rejection, laughter, and retreating footsteps echoing through the house.

But instead, after a long, tense pause, he said quietly, "I want to see them. The dragons."

Angelica and Christopher gasped. "He wants to see Qadira, Mama! He's not leaving us!" Angelica squealed, nearly bouncing out of her shoes.

Martina's eyes welled with tears. She reached out and took Marcus's hand, her grip both gentle and desperate. Christopher grabbed Marcus's other hand, grounding them all in a fragile, newfound trust. Angelica led the way, skipping ahead toward the cave, her joy echoing through the trees.

But Martina's heart still pounded, not from fear of what Marcus might do, but from what they were about to show him. The dragons were real. The past was real. And now, there was no turning back.

"This is… quite impressive," Marcus murmured, stepping closer and running his hand along the worn wood of the structure. "I wouldn't have guessed there was a cave in here."

Martina offered a faint smile, her nerves still simmering beneath her skin. "My dad and I spent months working on it. We wanted it safe for the kids. It looks like a shed from the outside, but underneath…"

She let the thought trail off as Marcus took another step forward, peering into the dimly lit entrance. A faint hum of electricity echoed softly, the wiring she and the GM had installed casting a warm glow along the tunnel's dirt path. The kids darted ahead, laughter bouncing off the walls as they skipped deeper into the cavern. Their joy was infectious, but Marcus remained silent, his expression unreadable as his eyes scanned the shadows above. He flinched slightly at a water drip echoing in the tunnel, eyes flicking upward. "I keep expecting something to swoop down on me," he muttered.

Martina chuckled under her breath, though her voice still had a cautious edge. "The dragons aren't here. They're in a different chamber. We call it the Big House. That's where they sleep, play, grow…"

Marcus nodded slowly. "The Big House," he echoed, almost to himself.

The deeper they walked, the more he struggled between doubt and belief. The idea of dragons, children raising them, and time-travel pushed the boundaries of everything he thought he knew. And yet, the warmth in Martina's eyes, the earnest wonder in the children's voices, and the strange electricity in the air made it impossible to dismiss all this outright.

Still, he couldn't shake the feeling that something was waiting beyond the next turn. "Come on!" Angelica called, her voice echoing excitedly down the tunnel.

"This way, hurry!" Christopher beckoned too, waving Marcus and Martina forward with both arms. "You have to see the nest!"

Martina felt her heart race as she followed Marcus, her eyes fixed on him, reading every flicker of expression. The air grew warmer as they moved deeper into the cavern, the walls glowing faintly from the heat radiating ahead. A soft, rhythmic hum, almost like a distant heartbeat, pulsed through the stone.

They stepped into the nesting chamber.

The room shimmered with a low, amber light from the hot coals that lined the nest in the center. Nestled in the glowing embers were eleven large eggs, each with a delicate shimmer, their surfaces veined with faint patterns that almost seemed to move. The air was thick with heat and something else, something more intense.

Marcus froze. His breath hitched when he laid eyes on the nest. "These… are the dragon eggs?" he asked, voice low, disbelieving.

Martina nodded, her pulse pounding in her ears. *Please*, she thought. *Please feel it. Please let one of the dragons call you.*

Marcus took a slow step forward. Then another. He circled the nest like a man drifting through a dream, his eyes wide and locked on the eggs. The children stayed silent now, their earlier excitement replaced with respect.

He paused before one silver egg streaked with a pale violet sheen. It pulsed faintly in the coals, almost as if breathing. "I… I feel strange," Marcus said quietly, pressing a hand to his stomach. "Something's wrong. My stomach feels twisted like it's in knots. And my head is pounding." He took a shaky step back. "We should go. I don't think I'm well. We can… we can come back another time."

He turned to leave but didn't. His feet wouldn't move. The pull was too strong.

"Wait," Angelica said, her voice hushed and solemn. "Are you getting a pain in your chest? And does your stomach feel like it's turning over and over?"

Marcus blinked, stunned. "Y-yeah… how did you—?"

"Mama," Angelica whispered, eyes wide with wonder. "I think he's feeling the dragon call."

Martina's breath caught. Marcus shook his head weakly, his voice hesitant. "No… uh, no. That's not what this is." But even as he denied it, his gaze returned to the silver egg, now glowing faintly beneath the coals, brighter than before. His dragon was calling, it was waiting for him.

Marcus's facial expressions were all they needed to know what was happening. He stepped forward, and Martina, Angelica, and Christopher looked on anxiously. Lala quietly entered the room and stood next to Martina. They all watched as Marcus tentatively reached out to touch the silver egg, worried he would get burned on the coals, but the pull was too strong. He lay his hand on the egg; it pulsed at his touch.

With trembling hands, Marcus lifted the silver egg from its nest of glowing coals. The warmth radiated into his chest as he cradled it gently in his arms as if it were something fragile. He turned to Martina and the kids, awe washing over his features, and he smiled a genuine, astonished smile for the first time since entering the cave.

Then he looked toward Lala, the ever-watchful owl perched silently nearby. Their eyes met. Marcus gave her a slow, uncertain nod. Lala blinked once and bowed her head in solemn response.

Running his hand over the smooth, veined surface of the egg, Marcus whispered, "This... this is impossible. Dragons haven't existed for centuries. This shouldn't exist. How can this be?"

Martina stepped forward, her voice calm yet electric with meaning. "Have faith in Goel," she said, "and all your questions will be answered."

Marcus exhaled slowly, nodding, though his eyes remained locked on the egg. The room seemed to hold its breath.

Then it happened.

A sudden jolt pulsed through the egg, so strong Marcus nearly dropped it. He gasped and stepped back as a loud crack echoed through the chamber. The egg shuddered again. A jagged line split across its surface.

Another crack. A shimmering claw pierced through the shell, followed by a snout of glistening silver scales.

The children cheered and clapped, eyes wide with wonder. The cavern was filled with light that seemed to come from nowhere and everywhere.

With one final push, the egg burst open and out tumbled a young dragon—sleek, silver, and radiant, his scales catching the light like starlight on water. His wings were small but strong, twitching as he raised his head and locked eyes with Marcus.

Time stopped.

Marcus dropped to his knees, overwhelmed. Tears blurred his vision as he reached out and the dragon pressed its snout into his palm. "Everyone…" Marcus whispered, his voice thick with emotion, "…this is Zakariah. Goel has remembered." The dragon let out a soft, musical chirp, and the air thrummed with ancient charm, old as time, new as hope.

Marcus and Zakariah put their heads together—they were bonded. Tears flowed from everyone's eyes. Martina felt a nudge on her arm and saw Rachid nestled next to her. Then Ashraf and Qadira approached the nest, ready to meet their brother. They approached Marcus, nudged his shoulder, and greeted their newest dragon rider. He looked up at the dragons as though he had known them his entire life. "Why was I chosen? I know nothing about being a dragon rider; what am I to do now?"

"You are not of the Derdjanian bloodline, yet the bond you and Martina share is strong," said Lala. "And so it will be when Angelica and Christopher marry; their spouses and children will have a dragon."

"Yuck, I'm never getting married," stated Christopher matter-of-factly.

"Yes, you are, brother; we must; all the dragon eggs must hatch," said Angelica. He looked at her and rolled his eyes. Everyone laughed and went to their dragons.

They spent most of the day in the caves. Martina stepped away at noon and returned with ham sandwich wraps, pickles, veggies, and drinks. She wanted Marcus to have as much time as he could with Zakariah before he left for Texas. Lala caught several fish in the pond for the new dragon, who devoured them. The other dragons were old enough to swim and catch their food; they loved to swim. Angelica and Christopher jumped into the pond and swam with the dragons. They had become excellent swimmers and could do many tricks with their dragons in the water. Everyone else sat and enjoyed the show. Marcus spent a week with Martina and the kids. Not only was it difficult for him to leave them, but it was just as hard to leave his dragon.

The day before Marcus left Loving, Martina's sisters, brothers, and their families, her parents, cousin Anna, and her family showed up at the house. Everyone showed up with a tray of food, drinks, or dessert in their hands. "What's going on? Why is everyone here? Did I forget we were having a party?" asked Martina.

"Don't you remember," said Gwynn, "you invited us weeks ago! Don't tell me you forgot to make the asado!"

"I'm sorry. I guess I did forget; I don't even know how to make asado."

Everyone set their trays in the kitchen and entered the living room. "Everyone, can I please have your attention?" said Marcus as he clinked his wineglass.

The room got so quiet you could hear a pin drop. Angelica and Christopher stood next to Marcus, and Martina's father stood next to Martina. Marcus pulled something out of his pocket and went down on one knee. "Martina, you and the kids have been a blessing in my life from the first moment I met you. Will you be my wife and children for the rest of my life and make me the happiest man in the world?"

Martina smiled, nodded, and wrapped her arms around Marcus. "I will marry you." Everyone cheered and clapped; they partied until midnight.

Marcus and Martina married within a month; he sold his house in Texas and moved to Loving. He tried to convince his daughters to move with him, but they were married and had families. Melanie's husband worked in the oilfield and didn't want to leave his job. She had a daughter named Thalia, who looked just like her—she was beautiful—and they would visit a few times a year. Kristie also brought her son, Kalon, to visit; he loved visiting the farm and spending time with Angelica and Christopher. Marcus didn't want to tell his daughters about the dragons; the fewer people that had to keep the dragons secret, the better.

CHAPTER SEVENTEEN

A few months after Marcus and Martina married, they went to the caves to see their dragons, which had become part of their daily ritual since the dragons had hatched—they now had four majestic dragons. Martina stood back with a warm smile as she watched the dragons interact with her children and Marcus, who might as well have been one of the kids when it came to playing with Zakariah! Laughter filled the air, blending with the deep, rhythmic thrumming of the dragons, a sound that echoed with pure joy.

Qadira, Rachid, and Ashraf, two years older and twice Zakariah's size, played as fiercely as he did. Yet, despite the difference in size, Zakariah held his own, diving into the rough play without hesitation.

Martina took it all in—the energy, the happiness, the unspoken bond between them all. It was a moment she wanted to hold onto forever. She decided to check on Lala and the remaining dragon eggs. As Martina made her way around the lake, she couldn't help but admire the stunning cave formations. The light danced off the stone, casting shifting shadows and warm glows, which was mesmerizing. The sheer beauty of it all stole her breath away. Martina felt at home in this underground world. Part of her even considered moving all their furniture down here, sealing themselves away from the outside world, just to keep her family safe.

As Martina entered the nesting room, she saw Lala sitting on a cot in the far corner of the cave. She stood when she saw Martina. "Are you feeling all right, granddaughter?" asked Lala.

At that moment, Martina felt the familiar pull in her chest, the yearning to be close to the dragon eggs, or at least one particular egg. She dropped to her knees and placed one hand on her chest and one over her stomach. "The coffee this morning didn't sit well in my stomach; I may have to break my fast and eat early," cried Martina.

"Lala, I'm getting a very familiar feeling."

Lala approached Martina. "Come now, come sit down on my cot and rest a bit."

"No, I need to go to the eggs." Lala helped her stand, and they walked around the nest. Martina stopped before two emerald eggs.

Marcus had entered the room and came closer; he put his arm around Martina's shoulders. He looked worried when he saw Martina reach out to touch the eggs. He reached for her hand to stop her. "What are you doing? You already have Rachid."

Martina looked up at Marcus; she hadn't ever realized he was there and felt like she was in a trance. "The egg is calling me; I must hold it." She laid her palm on one egg and then felt the pull of the other. Two eggs beckoned her. Why two eggs? At that moment,

Rachid was at her side, nudging Martina's belly. She pulled her hand away from the egg and petted her dragon. "What is it, boy?" He looked up at Martina, then leaned in, gently pressing his nose against the eggs. Martina reached out, placing a hand on each smooth shell. Marcus followed, resting his hands over hers.

"I can sense them," Marcus murmured, eyes wide with wonder. "You're right; the dragons within are calling to you." Their gazes met, sharing a moment of awe, and as if in response, both eggs began to crack beneath their hands. Martina gasped as the shells trembled, splitting apart right before their eyes.

"What does this mean?" Martina asked, turning to Lala. "Why are two eggs calling to me? Am I meant to have more than one dragon?"

Lala's eyes gleamed with knowing warmth as she studied Martina. A smile spread across her face. "You must be pregnant with twins. That's why two eggs called to you, or rather, to the children growing within you."

Martina's breath caught, her hands instinctively moving to her belly. Before she could respond, Marcus's voice broke through the moment, filled with shock. "Pregnant?" Marcus repeated, his eyes wide with shock. "I didn't know… Why didn't you tell me?"

Martina looked up at her husband, uncertainty flickering across her face. "I wasn't sure," she admitted. "I didn't want to say anything until I took a pregnancy test. But wait… it's too soon. I'm still pregnant. How is this happening before the babies are even born?"

Lala's gaze was steady, her voice calm. "Listen to your heart."

Martina hesitated, then closed her eyes, letting the powerful connection wash over her and praying to Goel for answers. The dragon pull was undeniable, strong, certain, and deeply affirming. Without another word, she picked up one of the eggs and handed it to Marcus. Lifting the other from the nest, she settled onto the ground, cradling the hatching egg in her lap as the shell trembled beneath her touch.

A heartbeat later, with a firm thump, the second dragon broke free. The shell shattered across Marcus's lap as the hatchling tumbled forward, its emerald scales just as breathtaking as its brother's.

Martina felt an undeniable certainty deep within her. This one was male. As she met his gaze, a name surfaced in her mind: Eman. She knew it instinctively, tied to his essence: faithful, strong, unwavering to his rider.

Another chirp drew her attention back to the dragon in her lap. With one final, determined crack, the shell gave way. Martina cradled its delicate yet powerful face in her hands. The dragon leaned into her touch, a wave of warmth and understanding washing over her. And then, clear as a whisper in her mind, it spoke. The dragon's name was Aasim, and she would protect her rider with her last breath.

Marcus scooted closer to Martina; they gently cradled the new dragons. Eman crawled out of Marcus's lap and curled up next to Aasim and closer to Martina's belly. Marcus raised his hands. "I guess no one wants to be close to me?"

"They want to be near the babies; I doubt if it's anything personal against you," laughed Martina.

"I'll go catch some fish for the new dragons," giggled Lala. She skipped off toward the pond. Martina sometimes felt Lala was almost childlike—awesome, but childlike.

Once the baby dragons woke up, Lala fed them the fish; she had caught two fish for each dragon. The babies devoured them and begged for more, so Lala went off to catch more fish.

CHAPTER EIGHTEEN

Martina decided to have a home birth since she wanted the twins' dragons to be nearby as soon as they were born. She enlisted the help of a local doula and prayed that nothing would go wrong. Martina feared the dragons would create a ruckus; even though they were small, they were still dragons and not to be underestimated. She spoke with Rachid, asking him to keep the dragons calm until after the birth. Once she had given birth, she planned to send Angelica and Christopher to fetch Eman and Aasim.

The birth of the twins, Madison and Mason, went smoothly. There were no complications, only quiet awe and deep relief. The room was filled with the soft, rhythmic breath of newborn life. They were identical, each with a crown of dark brown hair and wide, big brown eyes that blinked slowly at the unfamiliar world. Tiny, perfect replicas of one another, beautiful babies, and Martina's heart burst with love.

Marcus stood at Martina's side, his heart full. He bent over each child, pressing a tender kiss to their foreheads, his lips trembling with emotion. With a thick voice of gratitude, he whispered a prayer over them, words of protection, purpose, and peace, and then turned to Martina. Their eyes met, full of wonder and exhaustion that only new parents know. He kissed her gently, humbly, a quiet thank-you in every touch for her strength, love, and the miracle they now shared.

As soon as the doula left the house, the kids raced to the caves to get the dragons. When they returned, all five dragons came to the house to meet their newest riders. Aasim went straight for Madison; she curled up at her feet and looked up at her dragon rider. She purred so loudly that it made the crib tremble. Everyone in the room laughed with joy. The warmth emanating from Aasim's scales comforted Madison; she slept for several hours until Martina woke her for a feeding.

Eman padded over to Mason's crib, standing guard at its head, his sharp eyes watching over his dragon rider. After a moment of silent observation, he curled up at Mason's feet, his warm body a protective presence. Eman would be more than just a dragon; he would be a steadfast guardian and lifelong companion.

The baby dragons remained inseparable from the twins for several weeks, always close by. But eventually, Martina knew they needed more space to stretch their wings and grow. She finally sent them to the caves, where they could run, play, and explore freely.

Angelica and Christopher each cradled a baby dragon with gentle care, while Marcus and Martina carried the twins. As soon as they reached the caves, Eman wriggled out of Christopher's arms and leaped straight into the lake with an excited splash. Aasim was quick to follow, and all the other dragons soon plunged in after them.

"Qadira!" Martina called, her voice carrying across the water and echoing throughout the cave. "Watch out for the little ones!" Qadira, now towering at twice Martina's size, responded without hesitation. She swam gracefully toward the young hatchlings, allowing them to clamber onto her broad back, keeping them safe as they eagerly paddled through the water.

Martina and her family stood at the water's edge, watching the dragons swim effortlessly through the lake, their emerald scales glistening under the soft cave light. Ripples shimmered across the surface as the young hatchlings playfully splashed one another, their joyful chirps echoing through the cavern.

In Martina's arms, the twins slept soundly, their tiny faces peaceful. No one dared to make a sound, afraid to disturb the fragile serenity of the moment. Even the dragons seemed to sense it, their movements becoming more fluid and gentler as if respecting the quiet magic of the night. Marcus wrapped an arm around Martina, kissing her temple softly. Angelica and Christopher stood close, their eyes filled with curiosity as they watched the dragons. They were already forming bonds that would last a lifetime.

Martina felt an overwhelming sense of peace for the first time in a long while. She was surrounded by her family and their dragons and knew they were exactly where they were meant to be.

The months passed quickly; Martina began the twins' training as soon as they could walk. They started gymnastics, which helped them with balance and agility, and karate at the age of three for discipline and focus. Like Angelica and Christopher, the twins learned quickly, and their dragons watched intently, surveying each move.

The dragons dodged and parried along the sidelines, mirroring every movement made by Madison and Mason as they trained. Their reflexes were sharp, their instincts honed through endless hours of playful sparring. Each step and strike was met with swift reactions from their dragon companions, forging a seamless connection between rider and beast.

Marcus had transformed the main cavern into a fully equipped training ground. There was also a space where the dragons could sleep, eat, and play without restraint. By day, the cavern bustled with energy, filled with the sounds of claws skimming across the stone, wings rustling, and the occasional triumphant roar.

At night, however, the young dragons were granted their freedom, allowed to soar under the cover of darkness to stretch their wings. The older dragons, however, had grown too large to fit through the cave's main entrance, making their confinement more challenging. Determined to solve the issue, Marcus had taken matters into his own hands. Using dynamite, he carefully blasted a new exit through the rockface, leading out through a hidden waterfall near the river.

The area was camouflaged and fenced off to maintain secrecy, ensuring that no outsiders could stumble upon their sanctuary. Marcus also devised a clever solution to avoid drenching themselves each time they passed through the waterfall. An irrigation ditch gate was placed at the top of the creek. With a simple adjustment, the water flow could be rerouted, temporarily halting the cascade and providing a dry passage whenever the dragon and rider took flight at night. With the new exit, the dragons had the freedom they needed, and their hidden world remained safeguarded, protected, and thriving.

As the dragons grew older and stronger, everyone began to learn how to ride. The transition from horseback to dragon riding came naturally, partly thanks to their early experiences with horses. While controlling a horse had challenges, requiring constant physical effort, reins, and commands, riding a dragon was an entirely different experience.

With dragons, the connection was deeper and more instinctive. There was no need for reins or physical cues—it was all mental communication. The dragons could sense every thought and intent, and responded with remarkable precision. It was a bond that surpassed simple control, more of a partnership than anything else. The communication was seamless, the connection immediate, and it felt like the rider and dragon were two halves of the same being.

In truth, guiding a dragon through the air felt easier than managing a horse on the ground. The mental link allowed for fluid direction, and the dragons, responsive to their riders' emotions, adapted quickly. What was once a challenge with horses now felt like second nature as the family soared in ways they had never imagined.

The dragons doubled in size yearly; with the vastness of an elephant, they effortlessly carried their riders. Their wingspan was easily the length of a small airplane.

Marcus designed saddles that would perfectly fit each dragon. Once on the saddle, the straps gripped the rider's legs, and a seatbelt like a harness kept the rider from falling. Angelica and Christopher were the first to try out the saddle and harness.

They communicated mentally and verbally with their dragons, and their efforts were rewarded with a perfect flight. Martina would holler at the dragon, "Qadira, don't fly so high. Ashraf, stop flying upside down." It made Martina nauseous to think of any harm coming to her children, even though both were already taller than Martina.

But Angelica and Christopher were unbelievable on their dragons—they would fly circles around Martina and Marcus, swerving in and out of the caves, through the waterfall exit, and down the river. "Come on, Sis; I bet you can't catch me!" hollered Christopher.

"Oh, believe me, brother, Qadira and I can make you eat our dust; we just chose not to at this moment."

"You two, stop fighting and watch what you're doing," shouted Martina. "You could get seriously injured if you fall."

"Mom, we know what we're doing; besides, our dragons wouldn't let anything happen to us."

Martina knew they were right, but she wanted training time to be taken seriously. Especially since the twins would be allowed to fly on their fifth birthday, just around the corner. Madison and Mason rode their dragons around the backyard or in the cave, like they were horses; it was entertaining, and everyone enjoyed the show.

CHAPTER NINETEEN

One evening, while Marcus and the kids were practicing on their dragons and Martina took care of the twins, GM came over and asked if he could ride one of them. His curiosity was getting the best of him. "Dad, are you certain you want to try to ride a dragon?"

"Sure, why not? I used to be pretty good on horseback."

"Great, let me ask Rachid if he will let you ride him."

Without hesitation, Rachid dipped his massive head and bowed in full acceptance, his wings flaring slightly with pride. GM's heart pounded as he stepped forward; this was really happening. He'd watched Marcus and the kids mount their dragons countless times, memorizing every movement, every strap and buckle. But now, standing beneath the towering dragon with the wind picking up around them, it all felt impossibly real.

GM placed his hand on the hanging ladder Marcus had built and grabbed the first rung. Martina stood at his side, steadying the ladder with practiced ease. "You've got this," she said, giving GM a firm nod of encouragement. Still, as GM began his ascent, his hands trembled, not from weakness but from a storm of anticipation and raw fear.

Halfway up, he paused. The wind tugged at his shirt, and the dragon's size suddenly overwhelmed him. He looked down at Martina, his eyes wide. "Maybe this wasn't such a good idea," he called down, his voice tight. "I think I'm coming back down."

"No, Dad!" Martina called back instantly, her voice strong and sure. "Keep going; you're almost to the saddle. You can do this, Dad!"

GM locked eyes with her and gave the slightest nod, swallowing his doubt. *Okay. For them*, he thought.

He kept climbing, step after step, until he reached the saddle platform nestled between Rachid's shoulders. With a deep breath, he swung one leg over and pulled himself into place. The saddle was surprisingly comfortable, built for long rides and rough winds.

He steadied himself, then slipped his feet into the stirrups, tightening the straps with practiced fingers. He secured the saddle fender around his legs, then clipped a safety harness at his waist. Finally, he gripped the pommel and the curved horn before him, holding tight as the dragon shifted beneath him.

GM was airborne in heart and spirit for the first time in his life, even if Rachid hadn't yet left the ground.

"Dad, you've seen us ride before, but it's different from being airborne. Hold on tight and let

Rachid know when you are ready to come down, and make sure to move your body when he moves, okay, Dad?"

"Yes, I can do this," shouted GM.

The kids looked at each other and started laughing. "Grandpa, don't fall, and don't throw up on Rachid; he will get annoyed if you do that."

GM peered at the kids through squinted eyes and pouted his lips. "Rachid, take care of my father, and don't let him fall." Rachid gave a snort, then nudged Martina's shoulder with his snout. She rubbed the underside of his jaw and said, "Off you go; hang on, Dad."

Rachid took a few steps, flapped his wings, and was in the air within seconds. The expression on GM's face was priceless—it was a mixture of excitement and complete fear! The kids whooped and cheered as their grandpa gave off a *woohoo*, then, he took his hands off the saddle horn, raised them in the air, and gave another *woohoo*. Rachid took a sharp right turn; GM grabbed the horn and ducked close to the dragon. He looked so happy, Martina's heart soared.

After what felt like hours, Rachid landed, and GM tried to climb off. His legs were so shaky that Marcus held onto GM's shoulders to steady him. "Well, Dad, what did you think about your first dragon ride?"

"It was incredible! Can I go again?" shouted GM; everyone laughed.

Angelica hugged her grandfather, and Christopher patted him on the back. GM looked over at Martina and thanked her for allowing Rachid to give him a ride. "Dad, you have to thank Rachid, not me; he is the one who allowed you to ride him."

GM turned to the dragon, gently cupping his enormous face. "Rachid, I am honored by your approval. Thank you."

The dragon harrumphed, his voice deep and rumbling. "It was my pleasure," he said in Derdjanian.

GM, eyes closed, suddenly jerked his head up, his gaze snapping to Martina. "Who said that?"

Martina blinked, confused. "Who said what, Dad?"

"Who said, 'It was my pleasure'?"

Martina stepped closer, concern creeping into her voice. "Dad, that was Rachid. He spoke in the dragon tongue. Did you understand him?"

GM nodded rapidly, his expression still puzzled. "Yes, I understood him." Turning slowly to the dragon, he laid a shaky hand on Rachid's snout.

Rachid's voice dropped to a whisper. "Go to the cave. Your dragon is waiting."

GM froze, confusion flashing in his eyes, then terror. His knees buckled beneath him. He dropped with a gasp, hands gripping the earth, shaking like something cold had just passed through him.

Martina and Marcus rushed to his side, barely catching him. "What's happening?" Marcus asked, breathless.

Martina looked at Rachid, her face pale. The dragon met her gaze and spoke, its voice rumbling like thunder from deep within, "His dragon calls. It has waited long."

Martina staggered back, the truth hitting her like a blow. Tears welled and spilled freely down her cheeks. She turned to her family, her voice cracking with awe and dread. "Dad… Dad has a dragon. We have to go to the caves."

Angelica shrieked in excitement, "Let's go get your dragon, Grandpa!"

Marcus helped GM to his feet and headed toward the cave entrance. Rachid and the other dragons took to the air and flew to the river entrance to meet the riders inside. As GM entered the cavern, he turned and looked at Martina. "I feel strange; I think I'm going to be sick to my stomach."

"Dad, it's okay; you probably feel the dragon pull. If you need to throw up, then do it."

"No, let's pause for a minute and let me get my head clear and bearings straight." GM bent over and took deep, long breaths, his hands on his knees; he shook his head and sighed. "I'm not sure if I deserve to become a dragon rider; remember, I kept you from your destiny the first time around."

Martina pondered over her father's words, a knot of uncertainty tightening in her chest. He had concealed the truth about Lala and her destiny in a previous lifetime so long ago, yet that was all in the past now, a chapter closed. For years, Martina had prayed to Goel, pouring her heart into the one wish that had never wavered: that her father would one day have a dragon.

GM had guarded her secret well, never revealing the hidden world of caves and dragons to Martina's siblings or his own siblings. It was a world that had been his, Martina's, and her family's for so many years, tucked away in silence, away from the lives of those closest to him. And now, against all odds, he was on the verge of becoming a dragon rider.

Her father's dragon was calling him, and she would guide him through this. "Come on, Dad, your friend is calling."

The group walked around the pond, entered the nesting cave, and headed toward the dragon eggs. The heat from the coals and the eggs made the room feel cozy and warm; Martina loved visiting the cave and the dragon eggs. She felt at peace near the dragons that hadn't hatched yet; friends they hadn't met but would be the most loyal companions to her family. Martina snapped out of her sentimental thoughts and turned her attention to her father.

GM approached the nest; he turned and looked at Martina and Lala quizzically. "What if I burn my hands? Those coals look hot."

Martina placed one hand on her father's shoulder and asked, "Dad, do you feel a pulling sensation in your chest, as though nothing can keep you from that nest? Walk around it and see if you want to touch one specific egg."

GM cautiously walked around the nest, then stopped before a black egg. He couldn't take his eyes off it; as he reached out to touch the egg, he paused, then grabbed the egg with a nod and a smile. GM tentatively held the egg in both hands, then brought it to his chest and sat on the ground. "What am I to do with you, little one? Won't you come out so we can all meet you?" GM caressed the black egg and prayed to Goel, thanking him for such a wonderful gift and blessing. "I was happy when you and the kids' got dragons. Then, Marcus got a dragon, and I was jealous and mad. But Goel has heard my prayers and has sent me Berakah."

GM quickly looked up at Martina and said, "My dragon, his name is Berakah. He just told or spoke to me, or I'm not sure how I know, but Berakah is his name, which means blessing."

Martina sat beside her father on the ground and put her arm around him. Then Christopher sat on the other side and said, "Grandpa, your dragon can mentally communicate with you even from within the egg. What else is he saying to you?"

"He said he is coming now; he can feel my touch."

Everyone was silenced by the pecking from within the egg; several cracks appeared, then one solid break right down the center of the egg. Berakah's shiny black scales and dark blue eyes were mesmerizing. The chirrup that escaped his mouth sounded unusual for such a regal creature, but he was still a baby. Martina's father sat there in awe, speechless, as he and Berakah observed each other intently. Martina knew from experience that they were communicating with each other.

"All right then," exclaimed Lala, making everyone jump at her sudden utterance. "I'm going to catch fish for the new hatchling." They all looked at each other and began to laugh uncontrollably. Lala shuffled off, looking around for the fishing rod that GM had bought her. She would hunt fish for the first month after a dragon hatched; after that, they would catch their fish themselves.

Martina hugged her father and petted Berakah, who was already fast asleep on GM's lap. "Dad, I know you are seventy-one years old and may not be able to train in combat like the rest of us, but you can train in dragon riding. Rachid will teach you everything you need to know, and Goel will strengthen your body. Want to start archery training? It would be a good skill to have."

"Yes, I'll do anything to help my dragon. When will he be old enough to ride?"

"Not for five more years, Dad, but you can ride Rachid."

"Do you think I'll be a good dragon rider, and what happens to Berakah if I die before the coming of Goel? Will someone else be able to ride him, or will he die too?"

That was a question that Martina was unable to answer. The thought of her father dying or the fate of Berakah was something she did not want to think about. "Let's take it one day at a time, Dad. First, let's get Berakah some fish, then you can start training tomorrow."

GM nodded and held his dragon even tighter.

CHAPTER TWENTY

It had taken Martina fifteen years of college, but she was finally an internal medicine doctor. With just one more year to go before completing her obstetrics training, she was closer to fulfilling the dream she had nurtured for so long. She had always promised herself she would be the one to deliver her grandchildren. But she also knew that there was more to it. Soon, they would be living underground for who knows how long, and Martina needed to be prepared for anything, especially health complications.

An on-site doctor would be vital for serious issues and something as simple as a cold. It was crucial, given how isolated they would be, and Martina was determined to make sure she was fully equipped to handle any situation that arose.

When Angelica thought about her mother delivering her children, she often laughed and said, "Mom, I don't know if I want you delivering my kids."

"Why not?" Martina would ask, genuinely curious. "We don't want a stranger in the house when your children are born. Plus, I'm not sure how the dragons will react."

"Oh, yeah, that's true," Angelica joked, "they may eat someone!" Her sharp wit always left Martina laughing. But when it came down to the practicalities of birth, the reality of delivering at home instead of a hospital eventually won out. The dragons needed to be close to their riders, a commitment that could not be ignored. The topic was settled; home births were the only option with Martina overseeing the process.

The following year, when Angelica turned nineteen, she set out to meet Nate, certain beyond doubt that he was meant to be her husband. Martina had already revealed the truth about her future—that she and Nate would marry and have two children together. Since that moment, Angelica had guarded her heart with quiet resolve, unwilling to give it to anyone but the man she had loved so deeply in a life before this one.

In the quiet spaces of her soul, she knew with unwavering conviction that Theris and Bennett were meant to be born in this timeline. It wasn't just a hope—it was destiny calling, echoing across lifetimes, waiting to be fulfilled.

Angelica had already researched Nate on social media before their meeting. She knew he worked at a hardware store and still lived with his parents. After all, he was only 18, fresh out of high school, and preparing to enlist in the Navy. But none of that mattered to her. She wasn't just thinking about the present, she was thinking about the future, the life they were meant to build together.

Martina booked Angelica on a flight to Laurel, Mississippi, where Nate lived. Angelica was determined to have this meeting on her own, without help from her mother.

Now, standing in front of the small hardware store, Angelica's hands trembled. Her heart pounded so loudly that she could barely hear the cars passing behind her. Through the window, she spotted him at the register—Nate.

Taking a deep breath, she wrapped her fingers around the door handle. *This is it.* She pulled it open and stepped inside. The bell chimed overhead, but the sound faded when their eyes met. *Everything around her seemed to drift into slow motion.*

Angelica wasn't the timid girl she once had been. She was a confident, radiant woman, unafraid of fate and sure of her heart. She walked straight up to Nate, every step filled with quiet power. "I'm going to be your future wife," she said, her voice unwavering, eyes locked on his.

Something sparked between them, instant and undeniable. The air thickened with it. Over the next month, they were inseparable. Each day brought new discoveries, laughter, quiet moments that lingered, and a growing bond that felt unshakable. Nate would visit Angelica in New Mexico on the weekends or Angelica would fly down to Mississippi.

It didn't take long. Swept up in the current of something far more significant than chance, Nate proposed, and Angelica said yes. But she knew their story wasn't complete. Not yet. For Nate to have the life he was meant for and for their future to rise on the wings of something extraordinary, they would need Goel's blessing. And she would do whatever it took to make that happen.

Angelica made a bold and unwavering decision: she would take Nate to the caves, to the dragons, to the eggs, and she would pray that Goel would grant him a dragon of his own. Angelica wanted more than love for Nate.

She wanted destiny.

Angelica led Nate through the backyard, stopping at the old shed near the trees. She opened the shed door and walked toward the back wall, pushing against it. A hidden door swung open, revealing a tunnel in the ground, an entrance he had somehow missed during all his previous visits.

"How did I not see this before?" Nate asked, peering into the shadows.

"It hides from those who aren't ready," Angelica replied with a knowing smile.

He followed her down the passage, and the air grew cooler as they descended. The tunnel twisted and turned, and with every step, the world above faded further, replaced by something enchanted, something ancient and mysterious that whispered of forgotten magic.

Nate couldn't help but marvel at the surroundings, but suspicion flickered in his voice. "Are you sure there are dragons in this cave? Or are you just leading me to a dramatic death in a hole underground?"

Angelica stopped and turned to him, half-amused, half-exasperated. "Nate! Seriously?" she said, raising one eyebrow as she always did. "Just trust me. You're about to see something incredible. But first, stop talking and listen. Tell me what you smell… and what you hear. Really listen."

Nate rolled his eyes playfully, then focused.

They hadn't been inside for more than ten minutes when it happened.

Nate stumbled, one hand pressed to his chest. His eyes widened. "Do you feel that?" he breathed. "Angelica… I feel it. I feel *him*."

She froze, heart leaping. "Your dragon?"

He nodded, his eyes glassy with wonder. "He's calling me. He knows I'm here, and now I know he's here." His voice cracked with awe and urgency. "Please, Angelica. Hurry. I can't wait another second."

Emotions surged through her: exhilaration, pride, disbelief. He felt it. He believed. She'd hoped and prayed but never expected Nate to embrace it this deeply, this quickly. This was more than fate; it was his destiny.

Without another word, she grabbed his hand and they ran deeper into the cave toward the nesting chamber. Toward the heart of it all.

Toward the dragon that had waited lifetimes for him.

They reached the nest, where the seven remaining eggs lay in the bed of hot coals. Nate was amazed by the glow and warmth in the cave; he looked from ceiling to wall to nest. "My dragon is calling me, Angelica," whispered Nate.

"Okay then, go on, just like we discussed, walk around the nest, and you will know which dragon beckons to you," Angelica whispered back to Nate.

As he approached the nest, a pearl-colored egg snagged his attention. Nate reached out and touched the egg that glowed exceptionally bright for him. It shook at his touch. He cautiously lifted the egg and held it with outstretched arms, admiring it until a familiar crack sounded. The egg began to break in two. Nate went down on one knee, cradled the egg, and out came Khalil, his lifelong friend who would never disappoint or abandon him.

Khalil had green eyes that mirrored Nate's, and his pearl-colored scales sparkled throughout the room. He was a magnificent dragon! Nate wept from happiness and love as his dragon nudged him under his chin; their bond was instant. He knew this was his destiny.

CHAPTER TWENTY-ONE

A month after their wedding, Angelica and Nate returned to the caves to visit the dragons. Angelica, now pregnant with their daughter, Theris, couldn't shake the feeling that her unborn child was already connected to this curious place. Though she hadn't yet sensed the distinct call of a dragon egg, as Martina had when she was carrying the twins, something about the place tugged at her spirit, as if Theris already belonged to it.

They walked slowly around the mist-veiled lake, its surface shimmering with eerie reflections. Angelica's eyes landed on a familiar figure, Lala, seated quietly on the weathered bench, her owl perched beside her, fishing with silent precision. As they neared, they noticed a bucket at Lala's feet, already brimming with freshly caught fish.

"Hello, Grandmother Lala," Angelica greeted, eyeing the bucket. "What are you doing with so many fish?"

Lala didn't look up. Instead, she tossed another fish into the bucket and said, matter-of-factly, "Today, Theris's dragon will come. I was gathering food for the newest hatchling."

Angelica blinked, startled. She turned to Nate, who raised an eyebrow. With a small shrug, she said, "Okay… let's see if you're right. We're heading to the nesting cave. See you soon."

Lala only smiled faintly and nodded, her owl's amber eyes fixed on them as they walked away, unblinking, knowing.

The moment they stepped into the cavern, the pull was undeniable. They walked straight to the nest and their hands instinctively reached out to touch a yellow dragon egg, and as soon as they did, a powerful pulse radiated from within. The egg throbbed beneath their fingertips, alive and calling to them. Angelica and Nate exchanged a knowing smile just as the shell began to crack.

From within, a breathtakingly beautiful yellow dragon emerged. She had large, luminous green eyes brimming with knowledge and wisdom.

"Kamaria," Angelica whispered as if the name had always been waiting on her lips.

She lowered herself to the ground as Theris stirred inside her belly, reacting to the moment. Nate sat beside her, his gaze filled with wonder. Kamaria nestled into Angelica's lap, her warmth seeping through Angelica's skin, a bond already forming. As if sensing the significance of the moment, Qadira, a towering presence of strength and grace, came forward and curled up next to Angelica, her watchful eyes gleaming in the dim light of the cave.

Eight months later, Theris arrived, and her dragon was waiting for her the moment she entered the world. It was as if Kamaria had known all along, standing guard, ready to welcome her bonded soul.

Theris was as beautiful as Martina had remembered; dark, wavy hair framed her delicate face, and deep, knowing eyes took in her new world. She was the mirror image of Angelica, but she had her father's long, sweeping eyelashes.

As Martina cradled her granddaughter, her mind drifted to the past, to the first time she had ever held Theris. She had once believed that no love could surpass the overwhelming devotion she had felt for the sweet baby girl in her arms. Memories flooded back—visiting Theris in California with Marcus, taking her to the park, watching her tiny feet stumble across the grass as she giggled in delight. Those were some of the best moments of Martina's life, and she cherished them deeply.

Theris gazed sleepily at the faces surrounding her, her tiny fingers curling against the fabric of her blanket. The moment Kamaria lay beside her, warm and protective, Theris let out a soft sigh and drifted into a peaceful sleep. It was a bond that had existed before time, a connection unbroken, stretching across lifetimes.

CHAPTER TWENTY-TWO

Christopher was in his second year of college when he met Catalina. She was beautiful. Dark brown hair that cascaded over her shoulders, hazel eyes that seemed to hold unspoken wisdom, and a soft, quiet voice that carried more meaning than most words ever could.

When he told Martina about her, his voice was filled with certainty. "Mom, I only had to look at her once to know... she's the one."

It didn't take long for their connection to deepen. They started dating, and love followed soon after, effortless and undeniable. Wanting to share his world with her, Christopher brought Catalina home to Loving. He wanted her to meet his family, and Ashraf, his dragon. But there was something he hadn't told her yet.

The dragons were a secret he couldn't just explain; they had to be felt and experienced. If Catalina was truly meant for this life, if destiny had a place for her among them, then the moment she neared the caves and the dragon eggs, she would hear the call. And Christopher silently hoped that she would, as this would be a sign that they were truly meant to be together.

When they arrived in Loving, he drove her through his grandfather's farm, letting her take in the vast, open land. They stopped by the river near the waterfall's opening, where the water glistened under the afternoon sun. Then, he brought her home to meet his family.

As they approached, Catalina's eyes widened in surprise at the towering steel wall surrounding the homes. It was unlike anything she had expected. The security gate slid open smoothly, revealing a hidden sanctuary beyond the barrier—lush green grass, towering trees, and three sprawling homes, their warm lights glowing in the distance.

She turned to Christopher, still processing what she was seeing. "This is… incredible," she murmured.

Christopher smiled. "When Angelica and Nate got married, my mom built them a house here. And when I started college, she made one for me too. We all get along so well, we wanted to stay close to each other." Catalina was taken aback by the setup but chose not to question it, at least not yet.

As they continued driving, she took in the impressive layout: a large circular driveway, an enormous swimming pool shimmering in the sunlight, pristine tennis courts, and even a fighting arena strategically placed within the grounds.

Her brow furrowed in curiosity. "Is this… a resort?"

Christopher chuckled. "No," he said simply. "This is our home."

Catalina barely had time to process that before he parked the truck and led her toward the shed where the cave entrance was secretly hidden. The air grew cooler as they neared and an unfamiliar sense of anticipation settled in her chest. "What is this, Christopher, why are we here? Are you are trying to scare me off by bringing me to an old shed before taking me to your parents?"

"Before you meet my family, there's somewhere else I want to take you," Christopher said softly, his voice threaded with something she couldn't quite place, gentle, sincere… but laced with mystery. He met her eyes, steady and unwavering. "Please, Catalina. Trust me. Keep an open mind, and an open heart."

She studied him, uncertainty flickering across her face. There was a weight to his words, something unspoken but absolute. After a pause, she nodded.

They stepped out of the vehicle into the hush of early morning. The air was still, cool with a faint scent of damp earth. Without a word, Christopher led her down a narrow path to a large shed nestled among several sprawling live oak trees. The trees loomed like ancient guardians, their gnarled limbs draped with hanging vines, casting shifting shadows over the weathered wood.

Christopher paused at the door, then pulled it open with a groan of old hinges. Catalina blinked in surprise. Inside was not what she had expected; it looked more like a cozy gaming den than anything mysterious. A small kitchenette stood against one wall, a TV and gaming console neatly arranged, and a bathroom tucked into the corner. She hesitated at the threshold, a chill running down her spine.

Turning to Christopher, she arched an eyebrow. "Is this where you play your Nintendo?" she asked, half-teasing, half-wary. "Why would you bring me here before introducing me to your mom?"

Christopher chuckled, his expression unreadable. He gently took her hand without answering and led her to the back of the shed. He pressed against the far wall, and to her astonishment, a hidden panel creaked open, revealing a narrow dirt passage descending into a brightly lit tunnel. A rush of cold, earthy air swept over her like a wave. She froze. The look on her face said everything.

"What is this?" she whispered, her voice edged with rising panic. "Please tell me now before I walk out of here, Christopher. I'm seriously starting to freak out." But then, suddenly, something shifted. The fear that had gripped Catalina just moments before melted away, replaced by something she couldn't explain. A calm certainty. A quiet knowing. Whatever lay beyond that passage was calling to her.

And somehow… she knew her life was about to change forever.

They moved deeper into the tunnel, the air growing colder and heavier with each step. The only sound was the echo of their footsteps and the occasional drip of unseen water. Catalina hugged her arms around herself, the dampness crawling under her skin like a warning.

They hadn't yet reached the lake when it struck her—a sudden, overwhelming pull in her chest. She froze mid-step, eyes wide. She turned to Christopher, panic flickering behind her gaze. But he said nothing; he didn't need to. Whatever this was, he had expected it.

Without another word, Catalina followed the invisible force tugging at her soul. Her heart pounded as she moved forward, deeper into the unknown. The cave walls seemed to narrow around her, shadows twisting in her peripheral vision. They went past the lake and down several tunnels, then stepped into the nesting cave.

She stopped in her tracks.

The room glowed with an eerie, pulsing light. The dragon nest was at the center of the cavern, nestled in a bed of smoldering coals. Large, scaled eggs lay resting, but one, just one, seemed to hum with a living heat that reached out and wrapped around her.

Catalina gasped, stumbling forward. Her hands flew to her mouth as tears welled in her eyes. Fear and wonder battled within her.

"What is this?" she whispered, her voice cracking. "What's happening to me?" She turned to Christopher, her face pale. "Why do I feel this way? What does this mean?"

Christopher stepped closer and gently touched Catalina's shoulder, his expression soft but serious. "Are you okay?" he asked quietly. "Tell me what you're feeling."

But Catalina couldn't find the words yet. Her chest was tight, breath shallow as if the air around her had thickened. The egg before her pulsed with energy, and she truly felt it, watching her, waiting for her.

"Catalina," Christopher spoke, his voice barely above a whisper, "I didn't tell you before because I knew you wouldn't believe it... couldn't. No one ever does at first." She stared at him, heart thudding, waiting. "I—my family—we are dragon riders," he said, the truth heavy in his words. "Goel has blessed each of us with a dragon. We must protect Earth when the day of reckoning comes."

He paused, searching her face. "And now... if Goel blesses you with a dragon, if you accept it, you'll be one of us. You'll carry the responsibility... and the power that comes with it."

Catalina's mind raced, but her heart was still. She looked at him, really looked at him. And in that moment, despite the whirlwind of emotion crashing inside her, she knew one thing with absolute certainty: Christopher loved her and would never lie to her.

She didn't know how she knew; it defied logic, but in her heart, she was certain. *Dragons?* The word echoed in her mind: surreal and impossible. Yet the presence stirring within the egg silenced all doubt.

Something ancient had awakened and it was calling her.

Deep in her soul, Catalina felt it. She was being chosen. She wasn't just a visitor to this hidden world; she was becoming part of it. A dragon rider.

She turned to Christopher and nodded quietly, her decision unspoken but clear. He returned it with a small, knowing smile. Then, heart pounding, Catalina turned back to the egg that called to her, the egg that was already hers.

With trembling fingers, Catalina tentatively reached out toward the glowing purple egg. Just before her skin made contact, she hesitated, pulling her hand back instinctively. She turned to Christopher, searching his face for reassurance. He gave a slight, steady nod. Heart pounding, she gently placed one hand on the egg's surface. It was warm, almost hot, its texture rough like sharp stone, yet not enough to hurt. Deep and insistent, a strange ache bloomed in her chest as if something inside her was being awakened. She had to hold it.

Without another moment of doubt, Catalina cradled the egg in both hands and pulled it to her chest. The instant it touched her heart, she gasped; the egg pulsed with life and the shell began to crack. Light poured from the fissures.

A piece of the shell peeled back, and from within, a pair of gleaming violet eyes met hers. A low, musical purr vibrated through the air as the hatchling broke free, its tiny claws curling gently around her arm. Her dragon, Nasira, had arrived. Nasira's gaze locked with Catalina's, and in a soft yet rich voice, she spoke, not aloud, but in a language Catalina somehow understood.

Derdjanian.

Catalina's breath caught. Tears welled in her eyes, not from fear but from awe. She looked up at Christopher, overwhelmed and speechless.

He was already smiling widely, proud as if this moment had always been meant to be. Catalina had believed that the love she felt for Christopher was already the deepest she'd ever known. But now, as she looked at him with fresh eyes, her heart swelled with something even more remarkable. At this moment, she loved him more than she ever had before.

And then there was her—this newborn creature, fragile, powerful, eternal, whom she'd only just met yet felt as if she had always known. The bond was instant and overwhelming. The love she felt for her dragon was just as fierce and profound. Two hearts, one human and one dragon, had taken root in her soul.

Then, without a word, Christopher dropped to one knee. He produced a small velvet box from his pocket and opened it to reveal a ring. The amethyst stone glimmered in the soft, cave-lit glow.

"Catalina," he said, his voice thick with emotion, "I love you more than words can say. Will you marry me?"

She looked up at Christopher with the widest, most radiant smile spread across her face. "Yes! I'll marry you, Christopher!"

CHAPTER TWENTY-THREE

Christopher and Catalina were married soon after, their hearts full and futures bright. They continued their college studies, hand in hand, and every weekend was a joyful return to family—and to their beloved dragons.

Their greatest adventure yet arrived a year later: their son, Jeremiah. Martina beamed with pride as she welcomed another beautiful grandchild into the world. Jeremiah had his mother's warm hazel eyes and a crown of dark hair. From the very beginning, he was precious beyond words. Strong, healthy, and strikingly handsome.

Of course, his dragon had already begun its journey; its egg had cracked open eight months earlier for Catalina. Maheer, a courageous black dragon with eyes like midnight stars, had patiently awaited Jeremiah's birth. It was clear from the moment they met that they were destined for one another.

Christopher made the familiar walk to the dragon caves. Maheer had already doubled in size since birth, and Christopher found himself huffing with effort as he carried the growing dragon back to the house and up the stairs to his rider. When Maheer entered the room, the air seemed to shimmer with anticipation. Everyone gathered close, eager to witness the joyful reunion of the mighty black dragon and his oh-so-tiny dragon rider.

Maheer let out a soft, rumbling purr and gently nestled beside Catalina and newborn Jeremiah, his great wings folding around Jeremiah like a protective cocoon. Catalina smiled sleepily, her arms wrapped around her son. Christopher sat on the edge of the bed, his eyes shining with pride and love. It was a moment of pure magic, a glorious reunion woven from destiny and devotion.

Angelica had prepared a comforting meal downstairs while Catalina was in labor, filling the home with warm, familiar scents. The rest of the family quietly made their way to the kitchen, giving the new parents and their bonded dragon a few precious moments of peace, love, and wonder.

It wasn't long before the next grandson arrived.

Bennett arrived on a cold January morning. He was just as Martina remembered, with his dark eyes and light hair. He had long eyelashes like his daddy and a beautiful smile like his mamma. Her grandson was adorable; Martina had missed his handsome face. Bennett's dragon was named Kaidan, another black dragon—he was brilliant. His body shined so bright with diamond-looking scales. Kaidan purred when he met Bennett.

Seven months before Bennett's birth, Kaidan had hatched in Nate's arms; he was an enormous dragon for his age but very attentive. Nate knew Kaidan would be Bennett's best friend. The dragon curled up at Angelica's feet as she fed Bennett. Martina leaned in and kissed her daughter gently on the forehead. Then, the world around her seemed to slip away when her lips touched Angelica's skin. A vivid and undeniable vision surged into her mind. She saw Angelica sitting in the soft glow of candlelight, cradling two newborns in her arms. Beside her, Theris and Bennett sat quietly, their faces alight with wonder. The air shimmered with warmth, something ancient and powerful, a presence that seemed to hum through the very walls.

Two newborn dragons, radiant and unlike any Martina had ever seen before, curled protectively near the newborn children. A sharp breath caught in Martina's throat. The vision wasn't just hope and longing. It was certain. Angelica would be a mother again, there would be two more grandchildren, and two new dragons destined to join the legacy. Her chest swelled, and tears slid down her cheeks before she could stop them. The vision, fierce and luminous, clung to her heart like a promise etched in flame. Angelica's brow furrowed as she caught sight of her mother's face. She reached up and gently touched Martina's damp cheek. "Oh, Mom," she whispered, half smiling and half worried, "are you okay? What is it? Did you have another vision?"

Everything around Martina seemed to drift into slow motion. A weight settled over her shoulders—the kind that always came before the future revealed itself.

Martina smiled and assured Angelica that all was well. Her daughter was not convinced but was too tired to continue the inquiry. Martina smiled and was content to enjoy Bennett until the day the twins were born.

A year later, when Angelica realized she was pregnant again, she asked Martina if this had been her vision. "Yes, I saw you had delivered twin boys."

Angelica felt like she was about to pass out! "Mom, twins? Why couldn't you have a vision of me with a new dog or one more kid?"

Martina laughed. "It will all be okay; this is your destiny."

Six months before the birth of the twins, everyone followed Nate and Angelica out to the caves. They were excited to see which remaining eggs would be for the boys. As they approached the nest, Angelica immediately felt the pull. Theris sat on the edge of the nest and informed everyone that the burnt-orange dragon eggs would be for her brothers. She crawled into the nest, picked up the first egg, and handed it to Angelica. Then she picked up the next egg and gave it to Nate!

Theris was indeed correct! Both eggs began to hatch. Nate held Sayyid as his egg hatched, and Angelica had Sharif. Both dragons were burnt-orange-colored and their eyes were as green as emeralds. Once he hatched, Sayyid looked around at the room full of people and squawked. Sharif looked around and bowed; it was a very noble act. Theris stood up, looked at Sharif, then turned back to her family and said, "Sharif is pleased to be here, and he says he is ready to serve."

The new hatchlings resembled the other dragons, yet something about them was undeniably different. Their torsos were longer, more serpentine, and their tails bristled with fur-like spikes that shimmered in the light, twitching with restless energy. But it was their faces that truly set them apart. Elongated and regal, with high foreheads and flared nostrils, they bore an eerie resemblance to wild horses—if wild horses had razor-sharp teeth and eyes that glowed with archaic intelligence. The new dragons were a welcome addition to their rapidly growing family, each a living symbol of hope and legacy. Martina's heart swelled with joy at the thought of what was still to come—she could hardly wait for the day Angelica's twins would arrive, joining the next chapter in their extraordinary lineage.

On a hot summer day, the air hung heavy with anticipation as Angelica prepared to bring her twins into the world. Her trusted doctor, Martina, stood by her side, poised and calm, as always. James and Luke arrived strong and radiant, with dark blond hair and piercing green eyes that shimmered like cut emeralds, another blessing from Goel. Angelica had done remarkably well with the bathtub delivery, her strength unwavering until the end. Exhausted but relieved, she cradled both newborns against her chest, her arms curled protectively around them as she drifted into sleep, her breath slow and steady.

Martina stepped forward, heart full, eyes misting as she took the babies' tiny hands in hers. Joy bloomed across her face; her grandsons were perfect. After gently cleaning them, she passed the swaddled infants to Nate, who had already brought Sayyid and Sharif inside.

The dragons waited quietly, their golden eyes fixed on the new arrivals. Their stillness was admirable, as though they understood the moment's gravity. When Martina gave the nod, they approached slowly, lowering their massive heads beside the boys. Sayyid and Sharif nestled against them without hesitating, curling protectively around their destined riders.

The bond had already begun.

Martina walked out onto the back porch after the delivery of the twins and sat to rest; her family had grown significantly. She watched as adults and children trained, strong fighters. Martina was so proud of them all. Theris was incredible; she was only six years old but acted and fought like a teenager. She and Madison would practice with wooden swords; Theris held one arm behind her back and would lunge and parry, riposte, and then she would be silly and do a cartwheel!

"Theris! Stop messing around and focus!" Hanbashi, her trainer, would reprimand her.

Theris would respond, "I'm also a girlie girl and a gymnast, not just a fighter! It's hot, and I'm tired! Granny, have the twins arrived, and can we please have some lemonade and sandwiches?"

Martina loved when Theris called her Granny; she couldn't deny her a thing. "Yes, I can get you some sandwiches and lemonade; yes, the twins are here." Everyone yelped and whooped: the long-awaited twins were here! Hanbashi waved goodbye and left, and everyone else went in to see the new arrivals and to eat.

The following morning, Martina heard the unmistakable clash of bodies and grunts of effort echoing from the training arena. The space, built by Marcus, Nate, and Christopher, was an impressive feat of structure: concrete slabs forming the dueling ring, closed-cell foam mats lining the wrestling zones, and multiple towering hip-roof shade structures stretching high above, wide enough for dragons to glide under and observe.

Truth be told, the dragons rarely came out during the day. Summer heat meant naptime, and nothing interrupted a dragon's nap.

Inside the arena, Madison and Mason, twelve and already fierce, were sparring with Theris and Nate. The air cracked with tension and raw power. Martina walked over and sat at the edge of the mat, arms crossed, heart pounding as she watched the twins unleash their energy.

Madison moved like lightning. She seized Theris by the neck, pivoted hard, and flipped her backward. Theris twisted midair, managing a backflip just in time to avoid crashing onto the mat. Martina surged from her seat, her voice cutting through the arena like a whip, "Madison! That was too rough! You could've seriously hurt her neck!"

Madison whirled, flushed and furious. "Oh, so now we're supposed to go soft? I thought we were training to fight, not cuddle!" Her voice rose. "Why is it always Theris? You're constantly babying her. Everyone sees it; you love her the most!"

"Madison!" Martina's voice trembled with frustration. "That's not true!"

Mason stepped forward, arms crossed tightly over his chest, his jaw clenched. "It is true. You treat us like we're dangerous. Like we're always one step away from going too far. But Theris? She gets praise just for showing up."

Martina's breath caught. The accusation stung because she didn't know if it was entirely wrong. She opened her mouth to respond, but the arena had gone still. Even the air felt heavier, as if the dragons themselves were listening now.

A low, rumbling breath stirred the dust from the shadows beyond the shade structures. The dragons were awake. Though they remained unseen, Martina could feel their awareness pressing in, ancient and watchful. Their minds, always connected to their riders, now pulsed with concern and warning.

Madison's fists were still clenched, her chest heaving. Still, her eyes flicked toward the dark edge of the arena, where golden eyes now blinked slowly open.

Mason shifted uneasily beside her, his earlier anger edged with unease.

Martina stepped forward, voice softer now but firm. "This isn't just training. It's trust. It's control. If you lose yourselves in anger, you risk more than a match—you risk the bond."

The words hung in the air like smoke.

One of the dragons, a massive silhouette, moved just enough for the sunlight to catch on its scales. A quiet growl vibrated through the ground beneath their feet: Rachid.

They were listening. And they were not pleased.

The tension in the arena thickened like the air before a lightning strike. The younger riders stilled, suddenly aware that their emotions had rippled far beyond the mat. Madison's defiance faltered, her glare shifting from Martina to the dragon whose glowing amber eyes now locked onto hers—not with hostility, but with warning.

The other dragons followed suit, their forms slowly rising, scales clicking like armor, eyes glowing in hues of gold, sapphire, and crimson. Their presence wasn't just intimidating, it was overwhelming, a force of nature awakened by discord.

Mason took a half-step back, his jaw tightening. Ever seasoned and steady, Nate lowered his stance slightly, acknowledging the silent authority filling the space.

When she spoke again, Martina's voice was softer but powerful. "Do you feel that? That weight in the air? That's what happens when our hearts fall out of sync and anger drowns out the bond. The dragons don't just watch us; they mirror us. Feed off us. And they know when something is wrong."

The silence that followed was deeper than before, respectful, almost sacred. Even the dragons, now settled into the shadows, seemed to hold their breath again.

And in that stillness, something shifted.

Madison's shoulders slumped. The fire in her eyes dimmed, replaced by a flicker of guilt. She stepped forward, voice trembling. "I'm sorry, Mamma… I let my jealousy get the best of me," she choked, tears welling up. She turned to Theris. "Did I hurt you? I didn't mean to. I'm so sorry."

Theris gave her a soft, forgiving smile, the kind that only a child so pure could offer. "No, I'm okay," she said gently. "But I'm sorry you feel that way. Grandma loves all of us the same. She even loves the goats and the chickens the same!"

That earned a round of giggles, and a few voices chimed in:

"Yeah, she really does!"

"Even that mean rooster!"

The tension melted away like morning mist. Nate stepped forward, placing a steady hand on Madison's and Mason's shoulders. "Guys," he said gently, "Theris is only six. That's half your age. You've got to go a little easier on her, okay? You can be rough like that with each other since you're the same age."

The twins nodded, shame softening into understanding. And then, without a word, they opened their arms. The group folded into a messy, heartfelt hug, dragons rumbling softly in the distance, their approval silent but unmistakable.

Martina wrapped her arms around them all, drawing them close. "Alright," she said, her voice light again, "how about some breakfast?" A cheer erupted from the group, and the moment broke into laughter and light.

But as Martina turned and walked away, her smile faltered just slightly. Deep in her heart, she knew the truth, one she kept tucked away like an old photograph. She did have a soft spot for Theris and Bennett. How could she not? They were part of her first life… and now, part of her second.

Just then, Rachid's voice brushed against her mind, calm, steady, and strong as ever: "Don't worry. All will be well. I won't let anyone hurt our family."

Martina exhaled, the tension in her shoulders softening at the familiar warmth of his presence. She paused, eyes drifting back to the training arena.

The children were already sparring again, laughing, shouting, chasing one another across the mats with renewed energy. A smile returned to Martina's lips, gentle but laced with the weight of memory.

They were safe. For now. And whatever the past still held, she wasn't facing it alone.

CHAPTER TWENTY-FOUR

As the months passed, Marcus took no chances. He installed high-grade security cameras around the property's perimeter, motion-sensitive, infrared-equipped, and linked directly to their internal network. Nothing could cross the boundary without alerting them.

Martina approved of every measure, though seeing their sanctuary slowly shifting into a fortress unsettled her. Still, peace was fragile and the world outside had grown unpredictable. She had lived through loss before, and she wasn't about to live through it again.

She often found herself walking the fence-line at dusk, eyes scanning the tree line, ears tuned to every rustle of wind or distant cry. Her family was here—Angelica, Christopher, Nate, Catalina, Mason, Madison, the grandchildren, the dragons—and she would do anything to protect them.

But sometimes, in the quiet hours of the night, a darker question settled on her shoulders like a shadow. How far was she truly willing to go to keep them safe? She didn't know the answer yet. But something in her bones told her she might have to find out.

As summer faded into fall and Thanksgiving approached, Martina prepared to host the celebration. With the golden leaves swirling outside and a chill in the air, excitement and a bit of nervous anticipation filled her home. Angelica and Catalina were by her side, helping to tidy, decorate, and cook, ensuring that every corner of the house felt warm and welcoming.

This year's gathering would be the biggest yet—over fifty family members were expected. Hosting such a large group meant extra care, not only with the preparations but with a closely guarded secret. Whenever Martina and Marcus had guests, they ensured that the dragons remained deep within their caves. The risk of someone stumbling upon them was far too significant.

Only her immediate family and her father knew of the dragons' existence—the fewer people who knew, the safer the dragons would be. Martina couldn't bear the thought of someone harming them, or even fearing them. The dragons were fiercely loyal to their riders, but to outsiders, they could be unpredictable and even dangerous.

Despite the hidden weight she carried, the dinner itself was a joy. Everyone brought a favorite dish or dessert, filling the house with mouthwatering aromas of roasted turkey, spiced cider, sweet pies, and savory brisket. Laughter echoed through the rooms as Martina watched her sisters share drinks, crack jokes, and relive old memories. There was truly no place on

Earth she'd rather be than surrounded by her family. It was chaos, but the kind she cherished.

The following morning, the dragons stirred early, their hunger waking them before the first light broke over the horizon. Still groggy from the long day before, Martina rubbed her eyes as she heard the distant rumble of wings stretching and claws scraping the stone. It was time, again, for their meal.

With fourteen dragons to feed, their appetites were enormous. At least five cows were devoured daily by the dragons, and that was on the lighter side! Marcus had resorted to buying livestock in bulk, arranging monthly deliveries that made the ranchers raise their eyebrows, but he never explained. He couldn't.

He'd even hired a small crew of trustworthy men to build proper stables and corrals: one for cattle, another for goats, and pens for other livestock. They ensured the enclosures were placed at the very edge of the property, far from the main house. Martina had insisted; she couldn't stand the smell drifting through the windows on a windy day.

Still, even with all the logistics, she hesitated sometimes. Just briefly.

The cost was staggering, including feeding and maintenance. It all added up so quickly. But then she'd look at them, those massive, ancient beings curled up like overgrown house-cats after a feast, and feel the warmth rise in her chest. Thank Goel for the diamonds and gems hidden deep in the caves, for her grandfather's inheritance, and for the steady income streams from everyone else. Without that, none of this would be possible.

Yes, it was a lot. Too much, maybe. But it was worth it. Every ounce of effort, every coin spent was to protect what mattered most: her family and their dragons.

Once fed, the dragons would sleep most of the day, snoring softly in their hidden lairs, their bellies full and their minds at peace. Martina often watched them for a moment before heading back to the house, marveling at how something so powerful could look so peaceful. So… tame.

But come nightfall, everything changed. The dragons awoke with renewed energy, and the real magic began. Training sessions with the riders were breathtaking, equal parts chaos and elegance. It was dangerous, yes, and every session came with its risks. But it was also exhilarating.

And sometimes, just sometimes, Martina would find herself thinking: What are we really preparing for? But she never said it out loud.

CHAPTER TWENTY-FIVE

The temperature had soared to 105 degrees in Loving, New Mexico, keeping Martina and her family indoors for most of the day. But with evening finally settling in and the heat beginning to ease, they decided to head to Higby Hoe, their favorite swimming hole along the Black River. Tucked upriver from the central spot, Higby Hoe offered more privacy and less risk of being discovered. A full moon bathed the landscape in soft silver light, the weather perfect for a night-time swim.

Martina and Marcus took the younger kids and babies in their truck while the rest of the family traveled on dragon-back. Not far behind, Rachid and Zakariah followed, eager for an outdoor dip in the river versus the lake in the cave. Christopher built a small fire near the riverbank, its flickering flames casting a warm, golden glow across the water's edge. Catalina sat nearby, cradling Jeremiah gently in her arms while Maheer nestled close, his eyes reflecting the firelight as he watched the others with quiet curiosity. Nate paced the perimeter, flashlight in hand, carefully scanning the underbrush to ensure that no rattlesnakes lay coiled in wait beneath the moonlit shadows.

Everyone else had already plunged into the cool, dark water alongside their dragons, laughter echoing through the trees. Angelica had brought hot dogs and buns, and by the time Martina and Marcus arrived, she was already roasting them over the fire, the savory scent of sizzling meat curling through the crisp evening air.

Theris and Bennett clambered out of the river with help from their dragons, their hair dripping and smiles wide. They grabbed their food with eager hands, devouring every bite between breaths before racing back into the water, trailing laughter and droplets behind them like comets streaking across the night.

"Let your food go down before you get back in!" Martina hollered. But the breeze might have as well carried off her words; they were already halfway down the river, gliding effortlessly with a playful push from their dragons.

The evening was beautiful, the moon casting a soft silver glow over the water. The air buzzed with quiet contentment, the crackle of the fire mixing with the gentle rustling of leaves. Martina stretched out, wishing she'd thought to bring an extra blanket. A nap beneath the stars would have been perfect.

"I'm going to the big rock to dive off," announced Marcus.

"We're coming too," exclaimed Christopher and Nate.

"It's too dark and too late to be diving off there. Just stay here with the rest of us," hollered Martina.

"Don't worry, we'll be fine," laughed Marcus.

"Remember the rule!" yelled Martina. The men chuckled and continued to the big rock.

The only rule for diving off the big rock at Higby Hoe was to surface quickly to avoid hitting the muddy bottom, boulders, or getting trapped in submerged caves. The murky water made it difficult to see.

The thing about happiness is that it can disappear in an instant.

A few minutes later, Martina heard yelling— frantic, high-pitched, and full of urgency. Her heart dropped. "Mom, hurry! We can't find Marcus!" shouted Christopher.

She sprinted up the trail, dodging roots and rocks, her feet barely touching the ground as she reached the large boulder overlooking the swimming hole. Her breath caught in her throat as she spotted the worried faces gathered around.

"What happened? Where's Marcus?" she demanded, her voice already breaking with panic.

"He dove down and hasn't come back up!" Nate exclaimed, wide-eyed. "Zakariah and Rachid are searching but can't find him!"

Martina's heart pounded like a drum in her chest. "I'm a strong swimmer; I'll go look for him!" she said, already stepping toward the water.

"No," Angelica said quickly, grabbing her arm. "Let the dragons search. They can hold their breath longer, and it's too dark down there, the water is too murky; you won't be able to see anything."

Martina hesitated, torn between logic and instinct. Fear was clawing up her throat now, so she cupped her hands around her mouth. "Marcus!" she frantically screamed into the night. "Marcus!" Her voice echoed against the surrounding cliffs, then vanished into the still air.

Rachid surfaced moments later, mentally signaling as he looked toward Martina. Their mental link flared to life. *We can't find him. I've searched the main chamber and the ledges, but nothing. Zakariah's checking the caves, but he's worried. He thinks Marcus might be trapped in one of the tight underwater pockets. It's too small for us to reach.*

Martina's breath caught. The idea of Marcus being wedged alone in the cold darkness, lungs burning, was unbearable. She clenched her fists.

Should she call the police? Get divers and rescue teams? But all the dragons were here, glowing eyes, shimmering scales, wings tucked close. Authorities would ask questions. Too many. The weight of secrecy pressed against the rising tide of fear. Her husband might be drowning and she couldn't even ask for help.

"Keep searching," Martina whispered to the dragons, her voice cracking under the weight of fear. "Please, find him." She swallowed hard and then called out in her mind, *Rachid, go check on Zakariah now.*

Without hesitation, Rachid dove beneath the black, moonlit surface, his wings folding tight to slip through the current. The water closed over him with a silent gulp, leaving only ripples in his wake.

Minutes crawled by like hours.

Martina stood frozen, scanning the dark water, her breath shallow, her heart hammering against her ribs. She mentally reached out to Rachid, searching for his mind, for any trace of him, Zakariah, or Marcus.

There was nothing, just silence. Then, the earth jolted beneath them, a deep, violent tremor that rattled the nearby trees.

"Get off the big rock!" Christopher yelled.

Everyone scrambled, slipping on loose dirt and wet stone as they fled down the trail and off the boulder. The tremor grew stronger for a second, then suddenly stopped. An eerie stillness fell, broken only by the rising cries of the children.

And then, it came.

A deafening, otherworldly screech tore through the air, so sharp and raw that it seemed to rip the night open. The dragons' cries echoed from the water and the trees, rolling like thunder through the canyon. Everyone clutched their ears in pain.

Angelica dropped to her knees, shielding the twins as they cried in terror. Catalina did the same for Jeremiah, rocking him as tears streaked down his face.

But for the dragon riders, the pain was more than sound—it was felt. A searing, twisting ache exploded in their chests like something inside had been torn away. Martina doubled over, gasping, one hand pressed to her heart.

"No…" she whispered. Her knees gave out. She collapsed onto the damp earth, the horror settling in before the words could. The others felt it too. A collective wave of grief.

Marcus and his dragon were gone. Gone!

Rachid approached Martina, trembling as he delivered the devastating news: Zakariah had discovered Marcus's drowned body in a small cave. In a desperate attempt to save him, Zakariah had forced his way through a narrow opening, but as he did, the boulder above collapsed, crushing his head beneath its weight.

Martina crumpled to her knees, a scream tearing from her throat. "No, no, no… Marcus!" she cried over and over, her voice breaking with anguish.

Dragons circled like silent sentinels high above the river before diving into the depths to recover the fallen. Time seemed to stretch endlessly until, at last, the earth rumbled once more. From the churning water, Zakariah's lifeless body was raised.

Then came Rachid, rising from the river's surface with Marcus's limp body carefully cradled in his massive claw. He soared toward Martina, the beat of his wings stirring the air around her, and landed with surprising gentleness. Lowering Marcus's shattered form to the ground, he bowed his great head beside her, sorrow darkening his eyes.

The sight was too much to bear.

Marcus's body was nearly unrecognizable beneath the weight of the fallen stone. Martina's scream echoed through the valley, raw and unrelenting. Her grief was a storm, unstoppable and all-consuming.

The love of her life—her soulmate—was gone.

The weight of his absence settled over her like a crushing tide, drowning her in grief.

She stroked his hair, her fingers trembling, unwilling to let go. How was she supposed to wake up tomorrow and not find him beside her? How could she bear to walk through their home, see his things untouched, and hear the echoes of his laughter in every corner?

A sob caught in her throat as the reality hit her again: Marcus wasn't coming back. The warmth of his embrace, the way he whispered her name in the quiet moments of the night, and the life they had built together was all gone.

Tears streamed down her face as she clung to him, rocking slightly as if she could will him back to life. They were supposed to grow old together. They had made plans, had dreams of the future, watching their children build families, living underground with the dragons, and facing whatever came next—side by side.

But now, she would have to face it without Marcus.

A deep, mournful sound rumbled from Rachid's chest as he watched her, his golden eyes reflecting her pain. Even the dragon grieved with her.

"Mom," Angelica whispered, her own voice breaking, "we have to go."

Martina squeezed her eyes shut, pressing a kiss on Marcus's forehead. Her heart shattered anew as she finally whispered, "I don't know how to do this without you."

Christopher and Nate gently laid Marcus's broken body in the bed of the truck, then turned to help Martina climb up beside him. Her limbs moved on instinct, hollow with shock. Martina stared blankly ahead as the engine rumbled to life beneath her. The truck began its slow retreat from the place where her world had shattered.

The pain clung to her like a second skin. And at that moment, she knew that the hardest journey of her life was only beginning.

Once they returned home, the family gathered in quiet urgency, piecing together a story that could explain Marcus's death without arousing suspicion. They settled on a tragic accident. To support the narrative, Christopher tore down part of an old stone wall, originally built to block the scent of cattle from reaching the nearby homes. When the authorities arrived, they would point to the collapsed section as evidence, weaving their grief into a plausible lie.

Meanwhile, the dragons took Zakariah's lifeless body to the farthest edge of the property. There, under a canopy of stars, they honored him with a king's burial by fire. Flames roared into the night sky, casting long, flickering shadows over the land.

The family stood in sober silence, tears carving quiet trails down their cheeks as they watched the dragons mourn their fallen brother. Their grief was raw and essential, echoing through the valley in a haunting, echoing hymn. The sound, low and aching, lingered in the air like smoke, a sorrow that would forever live in the hearts of those who heard it.

After the funeral, part of Zakariah's ashes were buried beside Marcus, uniting them in rest as they had been in sacrifice. Martina honored Marcus's final wish to be buried, not cremated, and laid him to rest on the land he had loved, beneath the vast, open sky.

She visited his grave every day, as did the rest of the family. Some days, she sat silently, letting the wind speak through the rustling leaves. Other days, she talked to him, recounting stories, sharing her grief, whispering how much she missed him.

Time moved forward, but the ache remained. It didn't fade. It simply settled into her, a quiet, ever-present wound, a reminder of a love so deep that its absence would never stop echoing through her soul.

CHAPTER TWENTY-SIX

As the weeks passed, Martina settled into a routine, taking the grandkids to school, karate, gymnastics, and every other activity they were involved in. With Angelica attending college, Martina watched over the younger grandkids, ensuring that they were always safe and well cared for.

Angelica was on track to become a surgeon and was set to graduate the following year. The previous year, she had earned her degree in botany and horticulture and immediately put her knowledge to use, cultivating crops within the protective walls of their sanctuary. Every family member was assigned the duty of caring for the crops.

Angelica pushed the boundaries of her ingenuity, diving headfirst into hydroponic farming. If they were going to survive underground for years, perhaps even decades, traditional soil wouldn't be enough. Crop rotation could only go so far before the nutrients ran dry. But there was one resource they had in abundance: water.

She set up her system deep within one of the vast caves, stringing lines of tubing and growing trays beneath banks of ultraviolet lights. It was a gamble. But to her amazement, the results were beyond anything she'd hoped for!

Tomatoes swelled on the vine, their skins glossy and red. Jalapeños hung like green bullets, ready to pop. Fragrant herbs flourished in neat rows, their leaves vibrant and lush. The controlled environment, no scorching sun, no harsh wind, no pests, turned out to be perfect.

"Mom!" Angelica's voice rang through the cave, echoing off the stone walls. "You've gotta come see this! My crops, they've grown twice as fast down here!"

She stood proudly among the rows, hands on her hips, the soft glow of UV light catching the excitement in her eyes. At that moment, surrounded by thriving greenery in the heart of the earth, hope didn't feel so far away.

She assured Martina that when the time came, she would be able to sustain their entire family underground, growing enough food to survive the impending war. The thought brought Martina some peace, knowing they had a renewable food source, medicinal herbs, and the means to endure for years if necessary.

Angelica wasn't focused on just crops but was also experimenting with growing penicillin through a delicate fermentation process. It was a long shot, a project that could take months, perhaps even years, but she was determined. She tweaked the conditions daily, adjusting temperatures and variables and testing new methods. Failure wasn't an option. The stakes were too high and she couldn't afford to stop until she got it right. Every step, every adjustment, was a gamble for their future.

Even if their livestock supply dwindled to nothing, hunger would never be their downfall. The abundance of crops, fruits, vegetables, and herbs would more than sustain them. And if the world above crumbled into dust, they possessed the means to endure in the darkness below.

To ensure the longevity of their meat supply, the dragons entered months-long hibernations, reducing the strain on their livestock and preserving the resource for years to come.

Nate, Christopher, and Catalina had graduated the year before with engineering degrees, and their skills would prove vital in constructing the three-story underground tunnel system. Together, the family meticulously planned an intricate network to link their homes to the surrounding caves, an essential refuge for the uncertain years ahead.

The visions that haunted Martina and her children foretold a war that would ignite in seven years. When that time came, Martina and her entire family—including siblings, children, and loved ones—would be forced to retreat beneath the earth. There, shielded from the ravages of disease, famine, and radiation, they would prepare to endure the trials to come.

Before the project began, the time finally came for Martina to call a family meeting with her siblings.

Martina stressed the urgency of attendance. The following weekend, Angelica, Catalina, and Martina worked hastily, preparing a large meal for the gathering. The scent of roasted vegetables, seasoned meats, and fresh bread filled the air, comforting, almost distracting. One by one, family members arrived, laughter echoing through the house as plates were filled and glasses clinked.

But Martina's heart pounded beneath her calm exterior. She waited until everyone had settled and the room was filled with the soft murmur of conversation.

Then she stood up. "Thank you all for coming on such short notice," she began, her voice steady but edged with sincerity. The room slowly quieted. "There's something I need to tell you that can't wait any longer." She scanned the table. Her siblings' faces were confused, curious, and faintly skeptical. She took a breath.

"You've all heard the talk, the whispers, the idea that the end of times is coming. We've dismissed it as myth, prophecy, and fearmongering. But I'm here to tell you that it's real. And it's coming."

A ripple moved through the room, chairs shifted, forks paused midair.

"My family and I have made our choice. We stand with Goel. And we've begun preparing for what lies ahead. We've contracted a company to build underground facilities, not just for us, but for all of you."

Now, there were murmurs. Someone opened their mouth to speak, but Martina raised a hand.

"Before you say anything, know this: I have it on the highest authority—visions that have never been wrong—that there will come a time, not far from now, when this land will become uninhabitable. Disease. Famine. Radiation. The surface will be a graveyard. If we want to survive, we must go below. We must act before it's too late." Silence fell over the room, thick and heavy. Outside, the wind picked up, brushing the windows like a warning.

Martina's siblings looked around at each other, dumbfounded. "What are you talking about, sis? Why would we ever want to live underground?" said Willow.

"When that day comes, I think I would rather die than be holed up underground," said Magnolia.

Everyone in the room had their opinions and expressed them clearly. "Hold on, guys, we won't have to live down there forever, only until the air is breathable aboveground, then we can come out."

"Wait, so you're telling me that anyone that isn't underground will die because of radiation or bombs or become a zombie!" said one of the sisters.

Martina shook her head and said, "I'm not sure about the zombie part, but many people will die, and we will have to carry on and continue living. I want each one of you to understand the depth of my love and concern for your well-being. I am undertaking this project to ensure our safety when the time demands it.

"Construction is scheduled to begin in just a few days, and I'll keep you all informed about when you can visit and witness the progress firsthand. Remember, this project is a long-term commitment and will take several years to complete," Martina earnestly conveyed. A hushed silence descended upon the room as Martina's family members pondered their choice.

"There's no need for anyone to answer immediately," she assured them. "As we dive further into this project, I'll provide you with detailed information about living quarters and arrangements. But for now, I urge each of you to take some time for reflection and prayer, to consider your decision carefully."

Martina stepped away momentarily to give everyone time to consider the news. She entered the kitchen and began clearing the dishes when her sisters entered. "Martina, we have a few questions we need answered," stated Marguerite.

"Okay, go ahead," encouraged Martina.

"So, let's say that this event does happen in 'our lifetime'," she emphasized, "and we have been underground for a few years. What will become of us when we come out? Will the land be inhabitable? Will there be any other survivors? Will we all be alone for the remainder of our lives?"

Martina looked at each of her sisters and said, "Goel has given me visions of what is to come; yes, I know this sounds like I'm crazy, but these events will happen in a few years, and we all need to be prepared.

I have been preparing my children and grandchildren for years."

Martina related to her sister's concerns. She had been in the same place not that long before and realized that she would have to be more open with her siblings. "So, there is more to this story that I need to share with you all, but I'm not sure if the time is right. Also, I'm worried about how you will react and if I can trust you to keep this between us."

"Oh my goodness, Martina, just tell us already!" said Meadow. "We know you have been keeping something from us for years. Your kids and grandkids are like Viking warriors! What the heck are you preparing them for?"

Martina said a prayer to herself; she had kept the secret about her dragons long enough and it was now time to trust that her family would take it all to heart as she had. "It's best if I show you instead of telling you. Let's all go down to the caves and everything will be clearer."

"What do you mean, to the caves? There are no caves that haven't been covered up with boulders and rocks," said Lena.

"Do you all remember that I used to be obsessed with the caves and that I always heard a humming sound coming from them when we were throwing all those rocks in them?"

"Yes, I remember," said Magnolia, "you always said you felt a calling to the caves."

"Well," said Martina, "it's because there was a calling. When Anna and I were young, we went inside one of the caves." Martina narrated the story about her and her cousin Anna's venture into the cave. Her sisters listened intently and almost skeptically. "This next part is going to shock you so please listen before asking questions."

Martina continued the story about seeing Lala and her owl. "Oh, I remember you telling us that story about the owl talking to you," said Willow. "But that was a joke, wasn't it?"

As Martina recalled all the events that had occurred, including going back in time and redoing her life, she felt as though she was losing her sisters' attention. "Okay, now with all that in mind, let's go down to the caves, and I can show you the reason I was sent back, and I'll share the story of the prophecy," said Martina.

One of the sisters was about to say something but Martina promptly lifted her finger to her lips and said, "No more questions until you see this with your own eyes."

CHAPTER TWENTY-SEVEN

Most of the family had already drifted out to the pool, laughter mingling with the splash of water and the clink of glasses. The late-afternoon sun cast reflections over the surface, masking the unease that remained in Martina's mind.

Martina and her sisters walked around the side of the house, heading toward the shed where the entrance to the caves lay hidden. Shadows stretched long across the grass. "Can one of you go get our brothers and our dad?" Martina asked, her voice low but firm. "I want them with us when we go in."

Without hesitation, Lena nodded and hurried off. Minutes later, she returned with Lukas, GM, and Phillipe in tow. Angelica and Christopher followed close behind, their expressions uncertain.

"Mom," Angelica said, her tone cautious, "are you sure about this?"

Martina paused, turned to face them, and gave a solemn nod. "It's time. They need to see what we've seen. They need to know what we know."

She led them to the shed at the edge of the property then stopped just before the door and turned to face them all. Her eyes scanned each face, some curious, others anxious, and one or two already gripped by fear.

"What you are about to witness," she said slowly, "must never be spoken of outside this family. Ever. Do I have your word?"

A heavy silence followed. "Martina, you're scaring me," Marguerite whispered, clutching her arms.

"Well…" With a faint, uneasy smile, Christopher said, "…what you're about to see is kind of scary."

The siblings exchanged glances. Then, all eyes turned to their father, GM, who gave a slow, steady nod that was calm and reassuring but unreadable. Something in his eyes suggested he already knew more than he let on. "It's okay, everyone. Please listen to what your sister has to say," GM pleaded.

One by one, heads nodded. "We won't speak of it," said Phillipe. "You have our word."

Martina didn't respond immediately, but she pushed at the shed's back wall. Their surprised look was inexplicable when the shed's entrance led into the caves; without another word, she started down. All eyes scanned the walls and the ceiling and looked ahead to see what would come at them. Worry was evident on everyone's face.

Martina turned around and called her dad and children to stand next to her. "Everyone, what you are about to see will be unbelievable, but again, keep an open mind."

"I want you to tell us what we are about to see before you do anything else," said Gwynn.

Martina looked at her father and children with a questioning look and they nodded in agreement. "We have dragons."

Everyone looked at each other and started laughing. "Dragons?" They all said at the same time.

"Yes, dragons. Let's continue on," said Martina. As everyone continued walking through the tunnels, they couldn't believe they were even underground.

"Are you sure we aren't in some building?" said Lukas. "I've been in the caves when I was young, and they looked nothing like this."

"Well, we've done a lot of work, brother, to ensure that there would be no cave-ins." The damp smell came to everyone's noses and the cool breeze was obvious.

"It's so cold down here," said Meadow. "I wouldn't believe we were underground if it wasn't for the smell and the cool air. Feels like the Carlsbad Caverns."

They descended deeper into the cave and reached the lake. Martina turned around and reminded them about the dragons. She wanted everyone to remain calm and not let out screams when they saw the dragons.

"Come off it already," said Magnolia. "There aren't any dragons; we would have seen or heard them after all these years."

Martina looked at her father for support. GM stepped forward and spoke to the group, "Your sister is telling the truth; I was also blessed with a dragon and his name is Berakah."

Lukas looked at his father and said, "Dad, are you serious right now?" GM nodded and continued walking around the lake; everyone followed.

They stepped into the massive cave, and GM pressed his fingers to his lips, releasing a sharp whistle that echoed through the cavern. Martina quickly turned to her siblings, her voice firm yet calm. "No screaming. No running." They all nodded in apprehensive understanding.

A rush of wind stirred the air as the flying dragons descended from the shadows above. Martina, Angelica, and Christopher instinctively moved closer to Martina's sisters, while GM placed a steadying hand on Phillipe and Lukas's shoulders. No one dared to move.

Rachid landed with a mighty thud directly in front of Martina, his wings folding gracefully against his sides as his luminous eyes locked onto hers. The heat of his breath mingled with the cool air, and for a brief moment, the world fell silent around them.

Without speaking a word, Martina reached out with her mind. Their connection was instant and instinctual. *I've brought them here to meet you and the other dragons,* she told him.

Rachid blinked slowly, then bowed his massive head in solemn understanding. *They will be safe,* his thoughts echoed back to her. *No harm will come to your family—not while I breathe.*

He turned, lifting his head toward the gathering dragons. One by one, they had descended from the skies and now encircled the clearing, their bodies tense but still. With a low, resonant growl that vibrated through the earth, Rachid relayed Martina's decision. The others responded with subtle nods, low huffs of smoke, and quiet growls of agreement.

The message was clear: her family would be safe. But the air still held a tremor of something more—something unseen that had yet to reveal itself.

GM, Angelica, and Christopher went to their dragons and greeted them. Martina turned to her brothers and sisters and said, "These are the Derdjanian dragons, and they will help protect Earth and our family when the time arrives."

The dragons slowly circled the group in a slow, eerie motion. The younger creatures came around from behind, almost slithering along the ground. Even Martina got the chills witnessing their interactions. She sent a mental note to Rachid asking him what was happening. Her dragon responded: *A welcoming ceremony for your family.*

Martina glanced at the group and said, "Everyone, stay absolutely still; the dragons are going to greet you in their own way."

Gwynn's eyes darted anxiously from one sibling to the next, her breath quickening as unease crept into her expression. She took a step back, her voice sharp and unsteady as she turned to face Martina.

"I'm leaving," she said, shaking her head. "I want no part of this. I don't know what kind of game you're playing, Martina—but whatever it is, count me out."

Her words hung heavy in the air, cutting through the fragile sense of unity like a blade. For a heartbeat, no one spoke. Even the dragons stirred uneasily, sensing the shift in energy.

Martina held Willow's gaze, her heart aching with the weight of what she couldn't yet explain. But there was no stopping what had begun.

Qadira had already inched her way close to Gwynn, feeling her anxiety and fear. She made a clicking sound, and in unison, the other dragons began to click. Musical notes began to form from the clicking, hissing, and thrumming. The sound was beautiful and mesmerizing. All at once, the dragons took a deep breath and released it upon Martina's siblings. A warm, comforting, and soothing emotion spread throughout the room.

Martina saw a slideshow of her life: from the moment she had first discovered the caves as a child and had heard the humming sounds, to going back in time and her life from there forward. She glanced up at Qadira and asked, "What have you done?"

"We have breathed our essence, our very spirit, upon your family, and they will now know what your journey has been, and accept and understand our existence and our need for secrecy."

Martina fell to her knees, as did the rest of the group. "I am honored that you would bestow such a wonderful gift upon my family."

Lukas looked over at his father, tears streaming down GM's face. Martina realized from the look on her family's faces that everyone had seen the same memories. Lena was the first to speak, "I understand now why you have been so secretive for so long, Martina. Why didn't you tell us about it and let us share your burden? You should not have carried all this stress upon your shoulders alone. But what does this mean for us? What can we do to help, and will we be able to assist in protecting Earth when the time comes?"

Her family moved instinctively, gathering around Martina, Angelica, and Christopher. They embraced, holding one another tightly as tears flowed freely. At that moment, Martina's burden began to lift, no longer hers to bear alone but shared, carried together as a family.

"What's the next step? How can we help?" asked Phillipe, his voice steady but eager.

Martina opened her mouth to answer, but no words came. The tears still streamed down her cheeks and her mind spun too fast to form a coherent thought.

Angelica stepped in, her voice calm and resolute. "The next phase is to begin construction of our underground home. We mustn't think of it as a prison but as a retreat, a temporary refuge until Goel tells us it's safe to return above. Think of it as a home away from home."

She looked around at the faces before her, now attentive and alert.

"We'll install state-of-the-art cameras and a secure radio system throughout the area and nearby cities. Outside, we'll set up advanced sensors to detect radiation and other harmful atmospheric agents. Everything will be monitored constantly. But, most importantly, we need your silence. No one outside this circle can know about the dragons. Protecting that secret is key to protecting all of us."

A quiet moment passed, and then Martina's siblings each gave a slow, solemn nod. The weight of the truth had settled over them, but so had a renewed sense of purpose.

CHAPTER TWENTY-EIGHT

The following week, a construction crew arrived alongside the home inspector to begin a five-year endeavor. The project scope required numerous permits and rigorous inspections before, during, and after construction. Martina had spared no effort in assembling the right team. She hired an architect with experience in complex subterranean design, notably one who had worked on the underground development of the Waste Isolation Pilot Plant (WIPP), a facility known for its formidable engineering and security standards.

WIPP was constructed to dispose of defense-generated transuranic waste from Department of Energy sites around the country. The waste consisted of contaminated items containing plutonium and other radioactive man-made materials. It was permanently disposed of in rooms mined in underground salt-bed layers over 2,000 feet below the surface.

The difference in Martina's project would be that they would be mining in layers of impermeable granite; there would be no risk of contamination from radiation or any other exposure that could possibly kill Martina's family.

Nate and Christopher meticulously engineered the underground facility, with several strategically placed entrances designed to ensure accessibility and security. Just beyond the entry points, occupants would pass through a cutting-edge decontamination chamber, an essential safeguard against radiation and other environmental contaminants. This strict precaution stressed the facility's unwavering commitment to preserving a safe and sterile environment for every family member.

Five levels would be below the surface; the facility would be designed for survival and long-term comfort. It would be more than a bunker—it would be a home. Dedicated zones included a fully functional greenhouse for fresh produce, a gym for physical well-being, and multiple storage areas stocked with food, medical supplies, and other essentials. At the heart of the complex, a massive communal hall would offer enough space for a thousand people to gather comfortably, whether for meetings, celebrations, or moments of shared strength.

An entire level was designated for livestock, cattle, goats, and chickens, ensuring a steady supply of dairy, eggs, and meat. Christopher and Nate worked tirelessly to design an advanced air filtration and waste management system that would safely expel emissions without risk of contamination. Every detail and risk was considered and calculated.

The facility's water supply would be sourced from the underground river that flowed deep beneath the caves, an abundant and reliable resource. Advanced filtration systems would be installed throughout the complex, ensuring that not a drop of contaminated water could reach the occupants. As an added safeguard, backup generators were in place to activate automatically if the solar panel array failed, maintaining essential power without interruption.

Five hundred housing units would be constructed, each designed with comfort and functionality in mind. Communal spaces would be incorporated, allowing each family the privacy they needed to maintain a sense of normalcy.

The entire structure would be reinforced with thick, industrial-grade steel walls, engineered to withstand both natural shifts in the earth and any potential radiation breaches. Every inch of the facility was designed with soundness in mind, built to endure the unthinkable while offering its inhabitants a chance at life and safety beneath the surface.

The project took the contractors five years to complete. When it was finally done, Martina's siblings and their children came over to inspect the final build. What was once a simple shed concealing the caves had been transformed into a fortified fortress, a sleek steel structure equipped with a high-tech combination lock. Only a select few had access to the entry code.

Inside, the once-hidden panel leading to the caves had been completely overhauled. In its place stood an airtight steel door designed to prevent radiation leaks. Another intricate combination lock controlled access. Once sealed, the door could only be opened from the inside.

The tunnel to the caves had also been modernized. It veered away from the lake and was lined with stainless-steel walls, leading to a service elevator that descended into the newly constructed underground bunkers. There were also numerous stairways that led to each floor in the event that the elevators went out.

Although access to the lake and the natural caves remained intact, that section had been deliberately left unsealed—a calculated risk. The cave walls in that area were composed primarily of loose rock and porous soil, raising the alarming possibility that radiation could seep through over time. To mitigate the danger, Christopher and Nate took every precaution. They hauled in tons of additional stone and densely packed soil, reinforcing the entire area from above with painstaking precision.

The effort paid off, but not without cost. The narrow shafts and natural cracks that once allowed beams of sunlight to spill into the cave system were now buried beneath layers of reinforced earth. The gentle, golden light that had once danced across the cave walls was gone—sealed away with the sky above.

Now, the lake lay cloaked in shadow, silent and watchful beneath its fortified ceiling.

Different floors within the bunker were designated for specific purposes, each carefully planned to support the complex needs of life underground. The fifth floor was dedicated for the dragons. This floor was spacious enough to comfortably house all the dragons. It featured a sealed exit to the outside, equipped with a massive door large enough for the dragons to pass through once Martina confirmed that the surface atmosphere was free of harmful radiation. Another floor was designated for livestock, built to accommodate several herds of cattle, goats, chickens, and other animals.

The third floor was designated as the farming area, dedicated to traditional crops and advanced hydroponic systems to ensure year-round food production. Rows of artificial grow lights and climate-controlled zones would allow a wide variety of plants to thrive regardless of the conditions aboveground. Meanwhile, the first and second floors were reserved for housing, designed to accommodate all occupants and their families with comfortable living quarters, communal kitchens, and shared recreational spaces.

Martina, GM, and Isa were the first to enter the service elevator, along with twenty family members. Isa had finally agreed to join them in the bunker, though she made it clear she had no intention of seeing la bruja or the dragons. Her decision brought Martina a quiet sense of relief; having her mother there, even reluctantly, felt like a small victory.

The first group descended into their new underground home, and the next group arrived with Angelica and Nate, bringing with them a sense of excitement and curiosity.

Martina couldn't help but feel proud as she took in the finished structure. The years of effort had paid off—the space was functional, fortified, and thoughtfully designed. Her siblings and their children wasted no time exploring the housing levels, each picking out which rooms they wanted to claim as their own. Many rooms remained empty but had been intentionally built with the future in mind. The extra space would be useful if the family expanded, or if others were granted permission to join them underground.

Martina stepped back and quietly watched her family explore what would soon be their new home. A brief smile touched her lips as she took in their excitement, but it quickly faded, replaced by a shadow of worry. With the government unraveling and the threat of war looming ever closer, a deep unease had settled in her chest. Each passing day made the future more uncertain and her fears grew heavier. The signs were undeniable now: the uneasy hush in the streets, the way conversations died when certain names were mentioned, the quiet preparation happening beneath the surface. She knew the visions Lala had shown her were no longer warnings—they were inevitabilities. The Great War and the coming of Goel were upon them.

Lala had been clear: the war would leave devastation in its wake, with countless casualties on both sides. They would need skilled healers and medical professionals to tend to the wounded, but even that might not be enough. Martina's face had gone ashen at the thought of her loved ones caught in the crossfire. What if any of her family members were injured, or worse? The idea of losing them twisted her stomach into knots.

She couldn't shake the memory of Lala's voice, soft yet weighted with gravity: "Prepare yourself, Martina. Sacrifices must be made."

The stress of that warning settled heavily on her chest. She knew what was coming, but knowing didn't make it easier. All she could do now was brace herself and pray to Goel for the protection of those she loved.

EPILOGUE

Martina sat alone on the back porch, staring across the property toward the distant caves. The world seemed too quiet, too still, yet her mind was anything but. She didn't want to think about the future, war, or the unsettling possibility of living underground for years. The weight of it all pressed down on her, like a stone lodged deep in her chest. More than anything, she wanted to savor the simple joys of the present—her children, grandchildren, the dragons, and the life they shared. But there was always that dark cloud, the constant reminder of the chaos that loomed beyond the horizon.

A tear slid down her cheek, one she hadn't meant to shed. She wiped it away quickly, her hands trembling, when she suddenly felt a gentle pressure on her shoulder.

Theris stood beside her, her smile warm and steady despite the tension in the air. Without a word, she wrapped her arms around Martina's neck, pulling her into a tight embrace. The soft cascade of her natural curls brushed against Martina's skin as she held her close.

"Everything is going to be okay, Grandma," Theris whispered, her voice a soothing balm against the rising tide of fear. "Goel will watch over us, just like He always has. He'll guide us, lead us through the darkness. All we can do now is keep our faith strong."

The words were comforting, yet the quiet weight of uncertainty lingered. In the distance, the caves seemed to watch over them, silent and ominous, an unspoken reminder of the dangers that awaited. And yet, for a brief moment, Martina allowed herself to believe. Maybe, just maybe, the future wouldn't be as bleak as it seemed.

She stood abruptly, shaking off the weight of her thoughts, and turned to Theris. Martina gazed at her granddaughter, her heart swelling with pride. She brushed a gentle hand over Theris's cheek and smiled. "How did you get to be so wise, my little beauty?"

Theris grinned. "Well, you are my grandma, and I am a Basquez. And let's not forget, we have Derdjanian dragons." She winked before her expression grew more solemn. "But most importantly, Goel teaches us to love one another, just as He has loved us. Our family has always held onto that love, and that's what keeps us strong. That's why we will survive." She squeezed Martina's hands, her voice unwavering. "Have faith, Grandma. All will be as it should be."

Martina felt tears prick at her eyes as she looked at Theris, a deep warmth filling her soul. She pulled her granddaughter close. "I love you, Mija."

Theris hugged her tighter. "I love you too, Grandma."

She took her hand gently, her grip firm as she spoke, trying to reclaim some sense of normality, of control. "Let's go see our dragons again before it gets too late."

Theris' face lit up, a burst of youthful energy breaking through the tension. "Can we go for a late-night ride on the dragons? It'll be fun, Grandma, just us!" she exclaimed, her excitement impossible to contain.

Martina's lips curved into a bright smile, a flicker of the joy she longed to hold on to. "Let's do it. I'll race you," she said, her voice light but determined, the challenge in her tone sparking a sudden sense of adventure.

The air around them felt different now, brighter, with a sense of urgency and freedom only the dragons could bring. But even as Martina raced toward the cave, her heart quickened with anticipation and a nagging feeling settled in her stomach. The evening was growing darker, and soon, the shadows would be more than just a looming threat. They would become the world they had to face.

www.ingramcontent.com/pod-product-compliance
Lightning Source LLC
Chambersburg PA
CBHW041047310726
48978CB00011BA/460